BLACK IMAGES
IN BRITISH TELEVISION

THE COLOUR
BLACK

Editors
Therese Daniels
and Jane Gerson

BFI Publishing

First published in 1989 by the
British Film Institute
21 Stephen Street
London W1P 1PL

Reprinted 1990

Designed by Design for Change Ltd
and David Dunbar
Typeset by Columns of Reading
Printed and bound in Great Britain by
Courier International Ltd, Tiptree, Essex

British Library Cataloguing in Publication Data
The colour black: black images in British
    television.
    1. Great Britain. Black persons. Portrayal
    by television programmes
    I. Daniels, Therese
    II. Gerson, Jane
305.8′00941

ISBN 0–85170–232–5

CONTENTS

NOTE ON CONTRIBUTORS

STEPHEN BOURNE is a freelance journalist and is currently working in the TV Unit of the British Film Institute

ANDY MEDHURST is a freelance writer and lecturer in film, television and popular culture

KOBENA MERCER is TV and Video Officer in the TV Unit of the British Film Institute

JIM PINES is a freelance writer and lecturer

PREFACE

Therese Daniels and Jane Gerson

This book began life as programme notes to accompany a weekend event in May 1988 at Cinema City, Norwich. The event aimed to exhibit and evaluate black people's contribution to popular television, and combined panel discussions on minority broadcasting and opportunities for black people in television, with screenings and extracts from popular television during the past twenty years. During the weekend we examined the changes that had taken place in black representation in this period and tried to assess whether or not progress had been made.

The book is divided into three parts, each of which focuses on a different popular genre – situation comedies; drama series and serials; and soap operas. Each part is introduced by a specially commissioned introduction which attempts to draw out the underlying themes raised by the programmes and the debates which they have generated. In his introduction to the book, Kobena Mercer has supplied an overview of the representation of race on television and an analysis of the major issues surrounding it, including a deconstruction of the contradictions and limitations inherent in discussing black representation in terms of a simple positive/negative dichotomy.

In choosing the programmes featured in the book we have selected those which seemed to be most significant in terms of debates about race. The choice was also partly dictated by availability of writing on particular programmes. Whilst incidents involving race in such popular soaps as *Crossroads* were vivid in our memories, they had not, frustratingly and perhaps significantly, inspired press comment. Moreover, programmes most popular with viewers are not necessarily those most written about in a critical context. Whilst the tabloids might devote endless column inches to top-rated programmes and their stars, these do not further critical discussion and have been excluded on these grounds. Conversely some programmes, such as *Wolcott* and *King of the Ghetto*, which were not successful in terms of audience ratings, have excited long and heated arguments which have been represented in the book.

The selection attempts to give a cross-section of attitudes which are not, necessarily, endorsed by the editors, but which, we hope, reflect the range and nature of the debate. Writing about the programmes varies from the blandly promotional to the fiercely hostile. We have included fairly lengthy pieces from the *Radio* and *TV Times* which will remind or acquaint readers with the basics of plot, character and background. However it should be stressed that these sources are part of the marketing process rather than constituting critical comment.

Independent opinion, particularly that of black writers, has been, more often than not, strongly opposed to what the TV companies have offered. The experience of racism in daily life makes this commentary particularly intense. It is an area in which the accepted critical 'disinterest' of TV reviewers is rendered inoperable. There is a wish that the powerlessness which racism seeks to impose on the black communities be countered to some extent by the powerfulness of the representation of those communities on television. Consequently these images are expected to yield significant results. The high hopes raised, for instance, by the appointment at Channel Four of a Commissioning Editor for Multi-cultural Programmes has led, inevitably, to greater expectations (and greater disappointments) than experienced in other areas of television.

Some of the articles included may be found unpalatable for their implicit racism and others disturbing for revealing conflict within the black communities. All, however, contribute to a multi-faceted portrait of the evolving black presence in British television.

GENERAL INTRODUCTION

Kobena Mercer

During the 1950s two events occurred which, between them, transformed everyday life and public culture in Britain. One was the mass migration and settlement of Caribbean, Asian and African citizens from the former colonies of an Empire who came to the metropolitan centre to start a new life and rebuild a war-torn economy; the other was the mass installation of television sets wired-up and tuned-in to receive broadcasts from the BBC and the newly formed ITV network. What has been the relationship between these two histories? What is the current relationship between black people and popular television in Britain?

This publication brings together journalistic articles and critical essays on this relationship and among the variety of perspectives one thing is clear at least: that the relationship has been and still is a highly problematic one. The event on which this collection was originally based – a weekend of screenings and debate at Cinema City, Norwich[1] – was an opportunity to take stock of black people's involvement in popular television. There was a recognition that, in recent years, the representation of black people and other 'minorities' has begun to change for the better. There was a general view that the impact of Channel Four – with its official mandate on 'minority broadcasting' – has helped to diversify the imagery on offer, from news and current affairs to entertainment like soap opera, situation comedy and drama series. Black people seem to be more visible today on both sides of the camera. With its commissioning structure, Channel Four has expanded independent production for television. The eighties

1

have seen the growth of black independent film-making and more black people gaining access to professional positions in broadcasting institutions. At Norwich, there was a sense that things have begun to shift. But this was counteracted by a sense that many things had stayed the same.

Indeed when we consider the very recentness of such change in this thirty year history from the 1950s to the 1980s, what stands out is television's resistance to change. Under Michael Grade's initiative the BBC's critical self-examination – *The Black and White Media Show* – hastened acknowledgement of the need for change; but note that the title puns on *The Black and White Minstrel Show*, a popular variety programme that only ended, after much complaint, in 1978, a mere ten years ago. The sense of frustration and exasperation at this institutional inertia became apparent in the discussion of black representation during the Norwich weekend. One might note that the avowed racism spoken through the character of Alf Garnett in the BBC's highly popular *Till Death Us Do Part* in the 1960s has been modified in the eighties reworking – *In Sickness and In Health*. In this the

The Black and White Minstrel Show. Photo courtesy of BBC.

Ended after much complaint in 1978

2

black character, Winston, answers back. But even so, in the main, soaps, sitcoms and drama still tend to depict black people in overly stereotypical forms.

The debate on ethnic stereotyping however has become a kind of collective ritual of rhetorical complaint; in constantly circling back to the criticism of 'negative images' and 'misrepresentation' it has become a repetitive discourse, evoking a strong sense of déjà vu; a feeling that 'we've heard it all before'. At one point during the Norwich debate, Farrukh Dhondy (Commissioning Editor for Multi-cultural Programmes at Channel Four) suggested that we ban the words 'stereotype' and 'positive image' from the vocabulary of television criticism. Censorship is never a constructive solution and it probably wouldn't be very practical because racist stereotypes are not going to disappear just because we might stop using the words that refer to them. Nevertheless, Dhondy's polemic acknowledges the crucial point that the debate on stereotyping has got stuck in a rut and is in danger of itself becoming stereotypical. The historical relation between black people and popular television (or indeed other media in popular culture) is a great deal more complicated than can be imagined within the confines of the simple dichotomy between 'positive' and 'negative' images. All too often the either/or alternative between positive/negative acts as a cipher or code for moral judgements and it is this implicit moralism that has led to a stasis in debates on black representation.

Stereotyping is a process of selective perception by which the complex character of experience is filtered and simplified into fixed categories. Thirty years ago the concept was introduced into sociology to shed light on the formative influence of images and representations in shaping our expectations and interaction in the social world. Racism and ethnic prejudice have long been seen as classic illustrations of this process of simplification, as both entail rigidly fixed beliefs about racial difference. As Stuart Hall points out, the depiction of blacks in popular media is restricted to a repertoire of basic images – the slave, the native, the entertainer – as only certain traits and characteristics are selected for emphasis.[2] In a situation of scarcity, when these are the only ways in which black subjects become visible, the inference that 'all black people are like that' is encouraged, simply because of the lack of alternative images. It is this process of simplification and reduction, whereby television depicts only a fixed and narrow view of black experiences, that is at issue, not only because it denies the rich diversity and differences among black people, but also because it burdens each image with the role of being 'representative'. As independent film producer Mahmood Jamal has said, "Being constantly misrepresented in the media can make one unbearably sensitive to issues of stereotyping."[3]

If we agree that this is the essence of the 'problem', the importance of a collection such as this is that it provides a valuable opportunity to re-assess some of the various 'solutions' that have been put forward. It seems to me that, in general terms, there are three lines of argument in play. To the extent that each invokes the positive/negative image polarity there is a logic of simplification at work here as well.

The first could be called the reflectionist argument which holds that television is a 'mirror of society'. On this view television has failed to 'reflect' the multi-cultural character of British society. This was the conclusion of the extensive research report compiled by the Commission for Racial Equality.[4] To a point this is entirely valid. Black characters tend to be confined to minor or marginal roles in mainstream drama like *Minder* and *Brookside,* which purport a certain degree of realism. Alternatively, when blacks do appear in realist drama it tends to be as deviants or 'problem orientated' characters, either aggressively threatening or victimised into submission. In either case black roles tend to be ghettoised and stigmatised as abnormal or 'undesirable'. But the generic conventions of realism – i.e. correspondence with reality – do not apply to other forms of entertainment such as comedy or science fiction. Furthermore, the key problem with the realist argument is that even if television could achieve a one-to-one correspondence with the real world 'out there' the resulting picture might not be all that flattering either. Black communities are neither homogenous nor all sweetness and light: the demand for positive images therefore fails to acknowledge the contradictions and conflicts that exist within black communities as much as between black people and white society at large. One may concede that plausible and credible black roles are few and far between in popular soaps (note the departure of the entire original black cast from *EastEnders*), but on the other hand, if one aspires to realist

4

and naturalistic values, then televison should necessarily depict the 'negative' aspects of antagonism and unhappiness that also characterise life in a multi-racial society. Realist drama like *Boys from the Blackstuff* has successfully done so in describing working-class life.

Far from being a neutral or transparent 'mirror', television is a social institution in its own right. Even in news and current affairs 'reality' is never passively reflected but actively constructed via the decisions made in the selection and priority of issues reported as newsworthy. The second major line of argument recognises this. It could be called the 'social engineering' argument as it claims that, as a public institution, television is morally obliged to offer positive images of disadvantaged groups in order to motivate their aspirations and correct the distorted expectations of the majority culture. In this case television is called upon, not so much to mirror the real world, as to represent an ideal world of achieved equality. What it shares in common with the reflectionist view is an assumption that television has powerful 'effects' on its viewers, particularly children. In many respects the argument takes its cue from the view that television has become, not only our primary source of information and knowledge about the world, but also (considering the hours we spend watching it) a means of socialisation itself. Whether or not TV has replaced the teacher as a source of moral and cultural instruction, the major fault with this determinist approach is its notion of the viewer or audience as a blank page, easily impressionable and susceptible to imitating behaviour portrayed on the small screen. This is the reasoning behind much of the debate on 'sex and violence' on television. Its major weakness is that it ignores the fact that most viewers are selective in what they choose to watch; that most viewers are capable of distinguishing actuality and fiction; and that most viewers are aware of their ability to change channels or switch off.

The specific problems with the 'social engineering' argument with regards to race can be illustrated by *The Cosby Show* which has been received as a breakthrough for positive imagery. Over and above the laconic charm of Bill Cosby's performance, the focus of this sitcom is the nice, middle-class, Huxtable household where very little can disrupt the tranquility of their home. As black professionals (a doctor and a lawyer respectively) Mr and

Mrs Huxtable exemplify 'positive role models' for their children, and by extension, the audience. In contrast to the pathological view of black family life, the Huxtables embody the ideal norm of the happy family. The show has been criticised for its lack of realism, but this is beside the point. Even though there is a highly visible black middle-class in the US, the universal message implied by *The Cosby Show* is that the 'American Dream' of well-earned affluence is alive and well and easily obtainable through hard work and parental discipline. In this sense the fact that this is a black family becomes almost irrelevant as the values depicted in its ideal world are traditional (white) middle-class norms: there is nothing specifically 'black' about the culture and lifestyle of the Huxtables, and in this way, the positive image is revealed to be no more than an imitation copy of culturally normative ideals.

The Cosby Show. Photo courtesy of Channel 4

The Huxtables embody the ideal norm of the happy family

The reflectionist and idealist arguments focus primarily on the quality of television representations and the 'effects' of television on its audience. The third strand picks up elements of both, but focuses more directly on what is considered to be the central cause of the problem: the lack of employment opportunities for black actors, writers, producers and directors within the broadcasting profession. If this could be called the 'equal opportunity' argument, one would concede immediately that the institutional barriers that restrict equal access to television as an institution, play a major role in the reproduction of stereotypical imagery. Since the late 1960s the Equity Actor's Association has made repeated demands for 'integrated casting', that is the casting of Asian and Afro-Caribbean performers on the basis of ability rather than ethnicity. The success of the recent drama series *South of the Border* demonstrates how rich and exciting television can be when such creative integration amongst actors, writers and directors is able to flourish. Indeed, this exception highlights the rule: institutional resistance to change. Like many other corporate establishments, in the private and public sectors alike, British television has operated like a closed-shop as far as black practitioners are concerned.

Here, the demand for positive images has expressed the claim (that of the right to representation within public service broadcasting) of a community more or less excluded from the means of representation. However I would question the idea that the quality of black representation is guaranteed to improve once the quantity of black professionals in television is increased. Can it be assumed that just because an individual is black, she or he has a collective as well as an individual interest in changing the prevailing relations or representation? Paul Gilroy and Jim Pines have noted that stereotypical forms of dramatic realism and comedy have been reproduced, paradoxically enough, in the work of black film and television practitioners.[5] I'm raising the issue like this because it opens up an area obscured by the simple black/white dichotomy of the positive/negative opposition: the differences among individuals, groups, opinions and positions within the category 'black'. The term designates shared histories, struggles and common interests, but recent emotive and volatile controversies around programmes like *King of the Ghetto* (written by Farrukh Dhondy), or films like *My Beautiful Laundrette*

Elicited divided responses within the Asian communities

(written by Hanif Kureishi), have elicited divided responses within the Asian communities, for example. Black comedy programmes like *No Problem*, and stars like Lenny Henry, have also provoked ambivalent responses: does Delbert Wilkins (Lenny Henry's South London wide-boy character) represent the same old clownish stereotype or a fresh and witty representation of black British identity?

Two crucial issues are raised by these questions, concerning audiences and producers respectively. First, the positive/negative framework cannot acknowledge the ambivalence of the stereotype, that is, how the same imagery can elicit contradictory readings and responses. At the Norwich event an episode depicting an Afro/Asian marriage in the *Empire Road* series (directed by Horace Ove) did exactly that: while some saw it as an encouraging and empowering image of unity, others felt that the underlying narrative was 'racist' as the Asian and Afro-Caribbean families were constantly trading insults. This example illustrates, not only what literary critic Homi Bhabha calls the 'splitting' of the racial stereotype in 'colonial discourse'[6], but the fact that when different expectations are brought to bear on the image, different

8

interpretations are produced as a result. Thus, secondly, such expectations are also felt by black practitioners whether writers, actors, directors or producers, who, by virtue of their access to the means of representation, can often be perceived as the symbolic 'representatives' of the ethnic community from which they come. In a situation of unequal opportunity and scarcity, the few black people who are able to secure a place in institutions like television or film-making may experience an inordinate pressure to 'speak-for' black people as a whole. This of course is the classic problem of 'tokenism'.

In a recent *Network* programme on black representation, when Samir Shah (Deputy Editor for News and Current Affairs) was asked about the BBC's record on equal opportunities he protested that, "I wasn't elected to do that job".[7] Quite rightly he refused to take on the role of ethnic representative: in any case it is impossible for an individual to take on what is properly an institutional responsibility. The underlying problem here can be described in terms of the 'burden of representation' imposed on black individuals who have been able to make some professional headway into the institutions of media representation.[8] From the audience point of view, it manifests itself in terms of the black audience's high expectations of black performers, writers and producers, and often when such expectations are disappointed the charge of 'negative image' is heard. Similarly in conferences and public debates there is often an expectation that all aspects of the black experience should be covered: hence the complaint of being 'excluded' when certain points of view are not represented. In my view this is at the heart of the problem, because if every black image, event or individual is expected to be 'representative', this can only simplify and homogenise the diversity of black experiences and identities. In other words the burden of representation reinforces the reductive logic of the stereotype.

A necessary part of a solution, it seems to me, would be to multiply the points of access to the institution itself so that black practitioners are able to develop creatively. In place of the pressure to 'get it right' all the time, should be the recognition that black artists, like any artists, need the space to experiment and the space to make mistakes without being punished for it. The innovative strategies and directions of black independent film

9

and video workshops (many of whom are funded by Channel Four) have opened new possibilities for black representation emphasising the diversity of black identities and experiences and new kinds of cultural synthesis possible in a multi-cultural context. However, in the light of impending deregulation, the future of broadcasting as a social institution is in question. While it could be argued that black people, and others regarded as 'minorities', have not fared very well under the traditional public service consensus and that the deregulated scenario should be welcomed for the opportunities it will bring, it could equally be argued that in the competition for ratings and under the pressure to be popular, a non-regulated media will inevitably squeeze out specialist or minority tastes and push black representation firmly back into the ghetto again.

In the face of this uncertain future, I think there is an imperative to understand the past, which is also much more complex and contradictory than our received knowledge would have it. There has been a black presence in British television right from the very beginning – Paul Robeson and Louise Bennett contributed to BBC drama and entertainment as far back as the 1940s and 50s. In a sense the problem is not one of marginalisation, because black culture has always been integrated with popular culture especially in the field of entertainment. The image of the black-face minstrel has an iconic status in mass entertainment. The fact that this enduring image is one of the most offensive and unpleasant representations of black talent and creativity does not mean that we can dismiss or censor it. On the contrary, it demands that we unpack the burden of representation and open up the history of black people's role in popular culture for a more penetrating analysis. Research in this direction is just beginning. In the meantime this publication invites us to rethink and re-evaluate the terms in which we have conceptualised race and representation in popular television. It may help to clear the ground for fresh insights and arguments that will hopefully interrupt the same old story of stereotyping.

Notes
(1) *Black People in British Television* was held at Cinema City, Norwich on 13–15 May 1988 and sponsored by the British Film Institute, Channel Four, Anglia Television and Eastern Arts.

(2) See Stuart Hall 'The Whites of their Eyes: Racist Ideologies and the Media', in *Silver Linings*, eds. Bridges and Brunt (Lawrence & Wishart 1981)

(3) Mahmood Jamal 'Dirty Linen', *Artrage* Issue 17, 1987

(4) *Television in a Multi-racial Society*, Commission for Racial Equality, 1981

(5) See, Paul Gilroy's article 'Channel Four – Bridgehad or Bantustan?' in *Screen* V 24 n 4–5 July-October 1983, partially reprinted in this collection. Jim Pines offers a lucid analysis of sociological stereotypes in Horace Ove's *Pressure*, in 'Blacks in Films: The British Angle' *Multiracial Education* V 9. n 1, 1981.

(6) See, 'The Other Question: The Stereotype and Colonial Discourse', *Screen* V 24 n 6 November-December 1983.

(7) *Network* is produced by the BBC Community Programme Unit and the programme on 'Black Representation' was transmitted on 6 June 1988

(8) I have discussed this in relation to black British independent cinema in 'Recoding Narratives of Race and Nation' in *Black Film/British Cinema*, ICA Documents 7, ed. Kobena Mercer (Institute of Contemporary Arts/British Film Institute 1988)

PART ONE

LAUGHING
MATTERS

Situation Comedies

INTRODUCTION

Andy Medhurst

The serious political analysis of comedy is a tricky and rarely attempted business. It stands in direct opposition to a number of widely held assumptions about how comedy actually works. It is regarded by many with derision and suspicion, seen as an activity fit only for dessicated academic killjoys, a plot by the sombre and humourless to confiscate laughter, a paradigmatic knee-jerk of the cultural 'loony left'. In short, to analyse a joke is to render the once funny unfunny.

Comedy, seen from that perspective, must be a poor, fragile little thing, unable to withstand the slightest amount of analytical pressure. Hollywood dramas, soap operas, theatrical tragedies – all these seem to suffer no lasting damage from critical scrutiny, but the moment a joke is dismantled for a closer inspection of its mechanisms it somehow becomes impossible to reassemble it.

Underlying both those attitudes is the myth of the subjectivity of humour, best encapsulated in the deathless phrase 'it's funny because it makes me laugh'. Each 'me', however, is a social individual, a member of various social groups, a possessor of a set of beliefs and attitudes, and a key factor contributing to the success or otherwise of a joke is how that joke fits or doesn't fit with those ideological positions.

Comedy is, to put it mildly, political. If you want to understand the preconceptions and power structures of a society or social group, there are few better ways than by studying what it laughs at. Comedy is about power: there are those who laugh and those who are laughed at. When (outside the rather self-conscious domain of 'alternative' comedy) did you last hear a joke that began 'there was this white, heterosexual, middle-class, able-bodied man went into a pub. . .'? There are not, for example, thousands of jokes about mothers-in-law because mothers-in-law are intrinsically or 'naturally' funny people, but because in a culture which has certain assumptions about gender, age and power, the mother-in-law is a threatening figure, a potential danger to men (a castrating force, if you feel the need to adopt the language of psychoanalysis), and the battery of jokes deployed against her are one way of trying to defuse that threat.

One of comedy's chief functions, then, is to police the ideological boundaries of a culture, to act as a border guard on the frontiers between the dominant and the subordinate, to keep the power of laughter in the hands of the powerful. Yet at the same time, because comedy is nothing if not contradictory, humour can also be disruptive to the social order, a full-blown challenge or a persistent sniping from the margins, a force for the advocacy of social change, ridiculing power rather than re-inforcing it.

It is simply not possible to make definitive pronouncements on the ideological proclivities of comedy (though it can be done with certain individual comic texts, as is shown below). The laugher and the laughed-at are not fixed, immutable positions; there is always a significant amount of blurring, except in a few extreme cases. Comedy is too slippery, too wicked, too wily to ever be pinned down on the altar of ideological purity. It is far from uncommon to laugh at a joke whose politics, if examined with care, would be reprehensible, but the skilled delivery of a joke can whisk us through the stage of ideological considerations to the pleasurable pay-off of the punchline. This is not said to excuse racist or sexist humour, but to argue that comedy does not achieve its effects through content alone. To ignore the importance of factors like structure and timing is to blind oneself to the full complexities of the comic text and has its frightful logical conclusion in those dour acolytes of humourlessness who scuttle so regularly into Channel 4's Video Box.

Hence to sit comfortably back and declare that most situation comedies are racist is not, I would argue, a particularly constructive or observant statement. Given the culture from which they come, how could they be anything else? However, what useful critical purchase is gained by wielding that deadening rubber stamp of a word? To label a text as 'racist', nothing more nothing less, is not to open it up to productive analysis, but to propel it into the realm of the untouchable. As Alison Light has said, reviewing an exhibition of Edwardian visual culture,

> The narrative of blaming which can conveniently resolve history into a fable of villains and their prey leads to an absolutist politics, a politics of dogma not discussion. . . There is no such thing as a simply 'racist' or 'middle-class' picture (or novel, or music). . . Of course books, paintings, songs 'reinforce' and help create contemporary perceptions of difference, but how they are received and the responses they draw upon are manifold and contradictory. . . For me, the exhibition's use of the word 'racism' was an authoritarian one, assuming the political agreement of its audience and mesmerised by its own power, as though to say the word was enough.[1]

Till Death Us Do Part remains, even after more than twenty years, the best test case for some of the general points made above. Alf Garnett is one of the few sitcom characters who has achieved legendary status. He is part of television folklore, and is best known for being a walking repository of reactionary prejudices. There is a Garnett exhibit at the Museum of the Moving Image: visitors press buttons labelled with the names of social problems and up pops Alf on a video screen and delivers his opinions on that topic. It's a bizarre idea, representing the conclusive institutionalisation of this ghastly bigot as a lovable icon.

Watching a 1960s episode of the series is a chastening experience. The sheer virulence of Garnett's prejudices (racial and otherwise) is startling, and far stronger than anything heard on television today. The key question about Garnett, and it's a crucial one for the politics of comedy as a whole, is whether we are invited to laugh at him or with him. Johnny Speight has always claimed that he wrote Garnett as a monster so as to expose his bigotry to ridicule, and the characters of Rita and Mike (his daughter and son-in-law) are there for that explicit purpose. The problem is that Warren Mitchell's performance as Garnett completely overshadows those of Una Stubbs and Anthony Booth; he has access to an enormous vocabulary of abuse that is all the more striking because it had been hitherto absent from British television screens. A whole repertoire of anxieties and prejudices was being expressed for the first time, and with such bravado and forcefulness that the response was instant and massive. Whatever Speight's intentions, Garnett became a figurehead, and *Till Death Us Do Part* was the most popular television programme, in terms of ratings, in the mid-60s. It is, to say the least, highly doubtful that its huge audience was purely composed of people laughing *at* Garnett, despite his manifest stupidities (arguing at a blood donor's session that black people's blood should only be given to other blacks, since it might turn whites into 'coons', for example).

The crucial absence in *Till Death* was any recurring black character. Thus *Love Thy Neighbour*, made in the early 70s, is important. It used the standard sitcom device of squabbling neighbours as the basis for its racial disputes. Eddie Booth was the Garnett-figure, Joan his long-suffering wife, and Bill and Barbie their black neighbours. The premise of the series seemed to be that there was a 'prejudice on both sides', and attempted to prove this by having both men verbally abuse each other in virtually every episode. For white audiences, however, the resonances of 'sambo' and 'nig-nog' had far more weight than the corresponding 'honky'. The narrative also undermined the series' ostensible pretensions to equality, since it was the black couple who had moved more recently into the street, so that Eddie's anxieties about immigration and incoming were always rooted in fact.

The other sitcom staple *Love Thy Neighbour* employed, was the convention that when husbands are at war, their wives stay friends, and mutually raise eyebrows about their spouses 'silly' behaviour – and here was the true core of the programme's offensiveness. Racial conflict was reduced to the level of 'silliness', as if Eddie's racist behaviour was of the same order as Terry Scott's arguing about the height of a garden fence. It wasn't, and by its relentlessly jolly insistence that it was, *Love Thy Neighbour* lacked the bitterness and contradictions of *Till Death*. The latter, whatever its politics, was at least never so trivial.

If any sitcom does deserve the dismissive rubber-stamping of 'racist', it must be *Mind Your Language*. Set in an English language class, it reached some kind of new peak by including every recognisable non-British stereotype in every episode –

Indian, Pakistani, Chinese, Japanese, Sikh, Turk, Greek, German, etcetera etcetera. It had one joke: these-foreigners-are-hilarious-because-they-all-talk-funny-don't-they. As a B-picture comedy film from the 1930s it might have had more of an excuse for existing, but in a multi-cultural society in the 1970s its cheapness, its monotony and its sheer bare-faced ignorance had no place whatsoever.

Mind Your Language. Photo courtesy of London Weekend Television

Set a new peak in racial stereotyping

Less thoughtless responses to the 1970s came in sitcoms like *Mixed Blessings*, which treated the topic of marriage between a white man and a black woman. It was, perhaps inevitably, coy and patronising, but not quite in the *Mind Your Language* league. It's an interesting index of the precise contours of racial anxiety, however, that marriage between a black man and a white woman is still untested ground for British sitcoms.

19

The Fosters was the first attempt at a British sitcom with an all-black family. Timidity and eagerness to please were its main faults, though I have never been quite sure exactly where that eagerness was directed. Was it made to reassure white viewers that black families in sitcoms were just as bland as white ones? Or was it some kind of extended sop to black viewers? These questions have been asked more extensively recently, with the enormous success of *The Cosby Show*. This American series has reactivated all the debates about incorporation and tokenism. Are the breathtakingly bourgeois Huxtables an accurate representation of black family life? Or a model to aspire towards? Or an example of the smothering arms of white sitcom suburbia widening just a fraction to let in a family of *nice* blacks?

For my own tastes, the Huxtables do veer too consistently into unrestrained niceness; they can be, as a friend once put it, obnoxiously benign. Several people present at the Norwich 'Black People and British TV' weekend, however, spoke in favour of the series, seeing it as a welcome break from images of blacks in crime and police series or as the butts of white jokes in other sitcoms. "A problem-free zone" was one description.

The problem, surely, is that one series with a black family is not enough. *The Cosby Show* was not designed to be the carrier of so much analysis and so many expectations. It is smooth, painless sitcom in an American tradition that goes back to *I Love Lucy*. What is needed is a broad range of sitcoms with black characters, otherwise the kind of problems arise that have beset the representation of minority groups in soaps (one black woman in *Coronation Street*, one gay couple in *EastEnders*). Thus *The Cosby Show* needs to be seen as part of a spectrum that includes British series like *No Problem*, *Tandoori Nights*, (though obviously there are different traditions and issues determining the production and reception of sitcoms with Asian rather than Afro-Caribbean characters) Channel 4's most recent offering, *Desmond's*, and the extremely popular and successful Lenny Henry sitcom featuring Delbert Wilkins.

The final, general point I want to make is to do with the vexed question of stereotypes. *No Problem*, for example, was attacked by black feminists as reproducing gender stereotypes of black women.[2] I don't want to challenge or support the validity of that particular claim, but it is important to remember that without

Channel 4's most recent offering

*Desmonds.
Photo courtesy
of Channel 4*

stereotypes there could not be comedy. Jokes need an object, a butt, a victim, and that object needs to be easily recognisable to its audience. Hence the big-busted dumb blonde, the wrist-flapping gay man, and all the rest, persist because of their crude, cartoon recognisability. So-called 'alternative' comedy has not removed the stereotype, it has simply substituted a new set. A Channel 4 sitcom called *The Corner House*, made in 1986, should serve as an awful warning to those who would purge comedy of its stereotypes. Its politics (racial, sexual, social) were impeccable, but it tried so teeth-grittingly, desperately hard to be right-on that it forgot to include any funny jokes. Comedy can never be inoffensive. Attack and hostility are built into its very structure and the skill in producing good, successful political comedy lies in finding the right targets.

Notes
(1) Alison Light, 'Don't Dilly-Dally On the Way: Politics and Pleasure in the Edwardian Era', *History Workshop Journal*, no 26, Autumn 1988, pp.161–2.
(2) See Brixton Black Women's Group 'Opinion', *City Limits* no.126, 2–8 March 1984, reprinted in this collection.

TILL DEATH US DO PART

UP WHOSE STREET?

The BBC1 comedy series *Till Death Us Do Part*, rudely interrupted last week by the World Cup, is back tomorrow. It has worked wonders for the BBC and become the curse of Granada's *Coronation Street* (both 7.30 Mondays). *Coronation Street* dropped to tenth TAM rating in *Till Death*'s fifth week.

Johnny Speight writes it: hitherto he has spent a large part of his life scripting for Arthur Haynes on ATV – 500 shows in ten years. He comes from West Ham and has always wanted to "write something real about a cockney family". When he raised the idea of *Till Death* with the BBC about two years ago they were not keen. Then Frank Muir took charge of comedy and Speight was asked to do a trial episode for *Comedy Playhouse*. That was last summer, and it was a resounding success.

With the new series has come a social breakthrough in comedy. Characters actually make jokes at the expense of real political parties and there has been a whole edition about colour and race prejudice.

Speight has been campaigning for years for serious problems to be tackled through TV comedy. The BBC bought one such play, *If There Weren't Any Blacks They'd Have To Invent Them*, and then decided it was too hot to handle. Rediffusion snapped it up and decided it was 'too controversial'. Dutch TV screened it.

Observer, 17 July 1966

Steptoe's successor on BBC1 is Johnny Speight's *Till Death Us Do Part*, a series which has me neatly split into halves which the best psychological surgery seems powerless to reassemble. My friends are divided, too. Of two intelligent, cultivated young fathers, one won't allow the bairns to watch that grotesquely awful Garnett family, lest some of its vile manners rub off. The other thinks it is the biggest breakthrough in utterly radical, all-questioning social satire since Tom Paine.

Mr Speight is really a serious dramatist (though not a conspicuously successful one) who has hit upon this remunerative method of getting his message across while rolling us, or some considerable number of us, in the aisles. What message? I don't think it's really just a question, as has been suggested, of making the Tories look idiots; that is almost incidental. It goes much deeper. In this latest series, which is rougher and wilder than anything that has gone before, Mr Speight brings into question fundamental assumptions about God, the nature of religious belief, the psychic fabric of hypocrisy and humbug, and possibly other deep issues which I have forgotten or missed while fighting for breath. For it *is* funny, desperately funny. And the Garnetts *are* horrors, infinitely more horrific than the Munsters. Between revulsion and fascination, one is hooked. Incidentally, while much

Till Death Us Do Part. Photo courtesy of BBC

The Garnetts – infinitely more horrific than the Munsters

has been rightly said about the virtuosity of Warren Mitchell's performance as the awful Alf, too little praise has been lavished on Dandy Nichol's exquisitely judged Old Moo. The seniors make the juniors look like puppets.

Maurice Wiggin, *Sunday Times*, 15 January 1967

VIEWERS, YOU WERE LOOKING AT YOURSELVES!

The fascination of Alf Garnett, the monstrous hero of the BBC's *Till Death Us Do Part*, lay in his ability to act as distorting mirror in which we could watch our meanest attributes reflected large and ugly.

Like some boil on the back of the neck that one cannot resist stroking or touching, this social aberration demanded the nation's attention.

Some 18 million viewers – half of Britain's adult population – watched him weekly wallowing in the hates and fears and prejudices most of us have tucked away in some genteel niche of our psyche.

Alf's views on coons, kikes and wogs; his reflections on Labour Party politicians; his suspicion of anything new like transplant operations; his ignorant superstitions, his insensitivity to beauty, his blatant hypocrisy can be seen and heard most days in most pubs, factories and boardrooms in the land.

Even his conventional virtues – his faith, his patriotism, his loyalties – have all been acquired for the wrong reasons. His religion is motivated by fear of a vengeful God; his admiration of the Queen, by snobbery; his passion for West Ham, by a need for aggressive self-fulfilment.

Fortunately, there are few of us who possess all of Alf's bulging portmanteau of hates and prejudices. But it is only the saint among us who does not share at least one.

The difference between Alf and most of us is that he brandishes his decadent and violent ideas in the foul-mouthed linguistic setting that suited them best. He was too uncultivated and ignorant to realise that if he disguised them under a veneer of propriety they would have been acceptable in our best drawing-rooms.

Perhaps the most disconcerting aspect of Alf's existence is that he should be a member of the working-classes. Ever since Rousseau's 'noble savage', liberal humanitarians have believed that given the right social conditions, the best in humanity would emerge from the lowest orders.

They had long ago given up the middle-classes and the aristocracy as too corrupted by self-interest to ever strive unduly for a broadening of the human spirit.

It would be expected that a Prussian Junker like Ludendorff could be described as "a man blind in spirit. He had never seen a flower bloom, never heard a bird sing, never watched the sun set".

And it was natural that the epitome of a nation's xenophobia, narrow-mindedness, obtuse attitudes should have been that red-faced, bloated representative of the upper middle-class, Colonel Blimp.

But the proletariat was better than that. So the Russian Revolution and the Welfare State set out to prove. Well, we know what happened in Russia.

Could it be possible that decades of literacy, universal suffrage, full employment, trade union protection and governmental paternalism could spawn a monster like Alf Garnett?

Sadly, it is only too true. The millions who laughed at Alf Garnett weekly knew only too well that it was true. And it is in reminding us how far we still have to go before any Utopian ideals about ourselves and our society can be remotely realised that Johnny Speight's creation has succeeded in providing on TV both a chastening and enlightening experience.

No-one can deny that some of the recent episodes of *Till Death Us Do Part* showed signs of tired flair and exhausted imagination. But even the worst ones were funnier, more stimulating and more nerve-provoking than 95 per cent of so-called comedy.

The nation owes its creator, Johnny Speight, and its cast, Warren Mitchell, Dandy Nichols, Anthony Booth and Una Stubbs, a debt of gratitude. But when a series as significant as *Till Death Us Do Part* leaves the air, it is important that a critic investigates the nature of its going.

Was Alf Garnett pushed off the BBC or did he die a creative natural death? If Johnny Speight is to be believed, Alf was smothered by an artistic climate in which he could not survive.

"We have been irritated by a number of idiotic and

unreasonable cuts",: he said. "The trouble has been since Lord Hill's arrival at the BBC and I could be the victim of new policies. I would write another series for the BBC but only if this censorship was stopped."

What evidence then, is there that *Till Death Us Do Part* has gone too far in its use of unseemly language, its derision of politicians, the monarchy, foreigners, its shocking of sensibilities over such topics as religion, sex and the family?

Judged by viewing figures, only a tiny fraction of the nation has been shocked enough by the Garnett family to stop looking at them.

This has by no means deterred pressure groups, like the one of which Mrs Mary Whitehouse is secretary, from blazing away at the programme as a disgrace to the nation and a potential source of corruption.

Because in a comic discussion about the beginnings of man, the words "your bloody God" and "that rubbish, the Bible" were used, Mrs Whitehouse's association has demanded that the BBC be prosecuted for blasphemy.

In the event of a prosecution, would Mrs Mary Whitehouse or the BBC be right as to what shocks and disturbs the nation?

The BBC, in its *Talkback* programme, has provided some evidence of where viewers stand on programmes that its critics claim go too far in the way of permissiveness about language and taboo subjects.

An audience of 100, scientifically selected from the London area by an independent firm, represents a statistical sample of the population by age, class, sex and earning power.

On the right of TV to upset and occasionally offend the nation 80 per cent agreed that it had that right. Did Alf Garnett stimulate racial prejudice? 95 per cent said No. Were references to the Queen by Alf Garnett offensive? 97 per cent said No. Was there a need for an independent viewers' council? 92 per cent said No.

These statistics, then, would seem to put paid to Mrs Whitehouse's constant claim that her body represents a majority, or even a substantial number, of viewers.

An incidental aspect of this affair is the fact that so many commentators have assumed that Lord Hill's presence at the BBC has been responsible for this new censorious atmosphere. It may not be true – Lord Hill should let us know – but when Prime

Ministers appoint politicians to be overseers of our beliefs and morals, suspicions will always be there.

Milton Shulman, *London Evening Standard*, 21 February 1968.

LOVE THY NEIGHBOUR

Thursday's new comedy series, *Love Thy Neighbour*, packs a special charge. Written by Vince Powell and Harry Driver of *Never Mind the Quality, Feel the Width* fame, it is about racial prejudice – with a difference. It should make us laugh a lot. . . and think a lot, too. The TV neighbours are Bill and Barbara Reynolds (played by Rudolph Walker and Nina Baden-Semper) and Eddie and Joan Booth (Jack Smethurst and Kate Williams). The series is called *Love Thy Neighbour*. The neighbours are Bill and Barbie Reynolds, Eddie and Joan Booth. Eddie and Bill find themselves side by side in the same engineering works. And the simple, lovely, volcanic idea which makes *Love Thy Neighbour* anything but another over-the-garden-wall comedy is that Bill and Barbie are black, while Eddie and Joan are white. Of course the mine had been laid, the fuse primed. Without the awful Alf Garnett, and *Curry and Chips*, it is unlikely that black actors, however eager to advance their careers, would have agreed to go on the box to be called sambos, nig-nogs, chocolate drops and further sweet talk of racial prejudice. Because racial prejudice is what *Love Thy Neighbour* is, unremittingly, all about; and it's very funny.

Bill and Barbie are played by Rudolph Walker and Nina Baden-Semper. Both are from Trinidad, and both prove conclusively that black is beautiful. In the 11 years since he arrived here, Walker hasn't been back home, although his sisters visit him sometimes. These days he lives in Essex with his wife, Lorna, also black, and their 10-month-old son, Darren. A qualified compositor, Walker immediately got a job in London with a firm of printers. His bosses must have been rather nice, because he very soon caught the acting bug and became involved with Charles Marowitz and the Theatre in the Round, and, if they read this feature in that office of his, he says they'll probably laugh like hell. He couldn't go on slipping away from the works, so he managed to fall downstairs, got a fortnight off and rehearsed like mad for the St Pancras Festival. Marowitz encouraged Walker to go on acting, but he had cold feet and went back to printing for four years. It took three more years before he stopped bobbing about between printing and playing, tore up his union card and went full-time for the stage. He found himself largely in heavy drama, playing African presidents and such; there isn't that much funny stuff around for blacks to act.

It's Nina Baden-Semper's first comedy part, too, and she's working at it. Nina came to England when she was 11, went to school in Manchester and then studied dance and drama in Canada, specialising in the modern, Martha Graham school. She returned to England, wanting desperately to be a dancer. "But six years ago there wasn't all that interest in contemporary dance and I found myself in Joan Littlewood's *A Kayf Up West*. Then my agent started sending me after all sorts of parts, and here I am". She lives in south-west London, at Barnes – "It's getting rather chi-chi. I must move out to Mortlake." One of her brothers, Terence is Deputy High Commissioner for Trinidad in London, her brother Morris, a Captain in the Trinidad Army, went to the Royal Military Academy at Sandhurst, and her brother Max owns a garage in Ravenscourt Park, London. She has four sisters, too, and everyone in the family tends to have jolly Sunday lunches together. Nina Baden-Semper had bad nerves about Barbie. When she went to the audition, she said that she hoped the blacks were going to be treated nicely. "I was terribly rude and I was terribly surprised to be recalled". No-one else will be, since she's dead sexy and pretty with it. Her view of her and Walker's looks is simple: "If they hadn't made the black people good-looking, black people wouldn't have done the parts."

Neither she nor Walker has ever been offended by any of the Vince Powell and Harry Driver scripts. The director, Stuart Allen, says that if they were, there would be changes. Nina reflects, with some wonder, that they write so well in the Trinidad way. Walker was so excited after reading the first script because he thought: "Here are white men writing for blacks and there isn't a touch of the Uncle Tom" – the kind of black person who is conditioned not to resist white patronage. He says one of the most interesting aspects of *Love Thy Neighbour* is that Bill and Eddie (played by Jack Smethurst of *For the Love of Ada*) are on the same level. "My arguments are as silly as his".

Still, there could be a flash-point somewhere, although those clued-up old hands, Powell and Driver, have special gifts for verbal ping-pong which tends to leave the ball suspended inoffensively in mid-air. But insults – "Eddie", says Barbie, trying to explain, "believes in calling a spade a spade"; "the trouble is", says her aggrieved husband, "he calls me a spade", – and food taboos, declining property values due to blacks next door, race relations, or the black man's alleged sexual potential, are all meat for *Love Thy Neighbour*. Walker says it's not true by the way, what some people say about blacks, "I spend my leisure time playing squash". He thinks the programmes will achieve something more than getting guffaws. Nina says that mocking themselves – and that's what both black and white are doing in the series – will break down barriers. "Anyhow, whenever people insult me, and they do sometimes, I call them white pigs." As it happens, both she and Walker live trouble-free lives alongside white neighbours.

Love Thy Neighbour. Photo courtesy of Thames Television

Race prejudice up for laughs

"This show," says Stuart Allen, "is about integration. We want to cool things, and we think we're going to succeed." But no-one working on it is at all concerned with doing good by stealth; you don't get laughs like that, and *Love Thy Neighbour* will get laughs because it's a sharp, expert appraisal of what the market will stand. Even if new ground is being broken in the old way, it's still a first-time ever. The matter is combustible, and people will talk.

Alix Coleman, *TV Times*, 1972

LAUGH AT THY NEIGHBOUR

Is race prejudice a laughing matter? The answer is 'yes' and it has been clear at least since April 1972. It was then that Thames Television first put *Love Thy Neighbour* on the air. Each of the six episodes, whose re-run ended recently, was watched by 14 million people, and two of the six topped the ratings. It continues where *Till Death Us Do Part* left off. A further series will follow shortly.

Alright: so this particular form of black humour is regarded by the populace as good entertainment, which means it is regarded by advertisers as good for business. But is it good for race relations? The Race Relations Board has doubts. Tania Rose, the Board's officer responsible for education and public affairs, says: "I haven't met a black person who isn't offended to hell by it." When the series began she was invited to see the first episode in advance and found it harmless. So she agreed to write a welcoming piece for *TV Times* only to find a different episode used for the first actual broadcast. This one angered her because it gave the impression the Board would entertain a complaint from a white family that blacks intended to move next door. She offered to meet the writers and explain the Board's true function. When further episodes again upset her she repeated the offer. It was ignored. Tania Rose now considers Thames TV's attitude "very irresponsible".

The row has since blown up again, this time over clubs. Clubs have been a sore point with the race relations industry since an incident at the East Ham South Conservative Club in April 1969. An Indian, A S Shar, was refused membership because of his colour, and the Race Relations Board took the club to court. The

Board lost in the Westminster County Court, won in the Court of Appeal, then lost again before the House of Lords, who decided firmly that a club which genuinely elects its members is outside the Race Relations Act. The statutory test is whether members of the club are a 'section of the public', and the Lords held that even though it was a political club (to which members of the Conservative Party were elected almost as a matter of course), that did not mean its members were 'a section of the public'.

A dismayed Race Relations Board suffered further disappointment last year, when the House of Lords widened its previous ruling to include not only 'members' to a single club but 'associates' with a right to use the facilities of 4,000 clubs. These associates, numbering over a million, have the right to use any club affiliated to the Working Men's Club and Institute Union, but only subject to the rules of that club.

A black associate ordered drinks in the Preston Dockers Club, but was told to leave because the club operated a colour bar. Lord Diplock called this a "deplorable affront", but joined his four noble colleagues in upholding an appeal from the Court of Appeal (who had allowed the Board's claim) on the grounds that the one million associates were not a 'section of the public'. In law their reasoning was impeccable; in common sense it had the asinine quality so often detected by laymen in judicial decisions.

It is understandable that just now the Race Relations Board are sensitive on the subject of clubs. Not so the producers of *Love Thy Neighbour*: they are not sensitive at all. In a recent episode, the nub of the plot was that Bill Reynolds (the black neighbour) got Eddie Booth (the white neighbour) kicked out of the Caribbean Club, Eddie avenging himself by calling in the Race Relations Board. Harmless fun so far? Perhaps.

But the man from the Race Relations Board as depicted by Thames would be sacked on the spot in real life. He started by producing the wrong Act and reading out (as if it were still in force) a provision repealed seven years ago. He took Eddie's complaint seriously, though it was obvious that the ejection from the Caribbean Club was due to Eddie's usual insufferable ill-manners, and was not on racial grounds at all (his honky mates Jacko and Arthur were cheerfully allowed to remain). The Board's man threatened Bill with a criminal prosecution although the point of the Race Relations Act procedure is that it works by conciliation and, in the last resort, civil proceedings.

Finally, he twisted the knife in the Board's wound by acting as if those House of Lords rulings about clubs had never been given. Viewers not solely out for a giggle must have gained a clear impression that the law would come down with a thump on any club managers who excluded people on racial grounds. Not all watchers of *Love Thy Neighbour* have the attitude: 'I'm here for a laugh, don't confuse me with the facts'. Or is that too charitable an assessment of the viewing public's social consciousness?

I thought not, and wrote to Thames suggesting that, though they might seek to argue that the programme is a comedy programme and that it does not matter if in such a programme the law is inaccurately portrayed, there is another aspect: "The series is based on the problem of racial prejudice and is watched by a large number of people. As a result of this episode they will have a totally incorrect impression of the law covering this sensitive field . . ." I added that it is not the function of television stations to propagate misunderstanding of this kind and asked Thames to broadcast a correction.

Thames refused. They said: "The object of the series is, of course, simply to amuse and entertain and we believe it has, in fact, been remarkably successful in doing so. Such evidence as we have of public reaction to the behaviour of the two principal characters in the series seems to prove that they are now fully accepted as 'figures of fun', and that no exception is taken to their absurdly exaggerated notions of racial prejudice."

Fair enough so far. To bring an explosive subject within the field where it can be made fun of is to defuse it, and that would be an important achievement. But then Thames gets on to less confident ground: "We fully accept your point that the portion of the programme dealing with the officer of the Race Relations Board and the incident at the Caribbean Club did not give an accurate impression of the law relating to racial discrimination. The original script was amended slightly so as to reduce the inaccuracy as far as possible but to alter it sufficiently to bring it fully into line with the correct legal position would have *destroyed the whole point of the programme* and this we did not feel we should do."

Now this is a striking admission. The *whole point* of an episode watched by 14 million people turned on deliberate misrepresentation of the law governing racial prejudice. Thames want to equate the Race Relations Board conciliator with the Gas Board inspector. Who cares if some comedy sketch misrepresents the functions of the Gas Board? But those functions don't impinge on the deepest feelings of many citizens. When the hurts of rejection, the despondency of exclusion, are in issue should the powerful TV medium travesty a law so recently and controversially enacted by parliament? That leads into deep questions about the social responsibility of television. Race is not the only sensitive subject. Can we accept the fencing off of a large area labelled: 'Humour' – suspend our belief and take no notice of the facts? I doubt it, and so does Sir Geoffrey Wilson, chairman of the Race Relations Board. Lenny Bruce proved the potent social force of humour, and it is Sir Geoffrey and his colleagues who face the backlash here. I asked him how he viewed the argument with Thames. He said: "I find this contempt for its social responsibilities by a major television network very sad. Obviously on this issue they are not prepared to strike a balance between television ratings and morality."

The impression strengthens that television regards race prejudice as up for laughs. The BBC have now joined in with *The Melting Pot*, described by one critic, Clive James, as "the worst thing for race relations since Pharaoh went sour on the Israelites". He adds that it would make "a terrific series".

Francis Bennion, *New Society*, 31 July 1975

THE FOSTERS

PUSHED INTO STARDOM BY A SCHOOLGIRL

Lenny Henry's Mum stands shoulder to shoulder with her 6ft. 2in. son. She makes a fine figure in her brown and gold lamé full-length dress, a Jamaican Queen of Tonga. Winnie owns the Henry family's large, crumbling Victorian corner house in Dudley, in the West Midlands, and it was she who came over here in 1958, found herself a job and the family a flat – and then sent for Dad and the rest of the family.

"What have you got on? You look as if you've been wallpapered back and front", barracks Lenny, who plays Sonny in *The Fosters*, the Friday comedy series. Lenny, aged 17, was born and bred in, as he puts it, the Black Country. "You know, people come up to me and ask me if I'm Lenny Henry. When I eventually say yes, all they say is: 'We've heard a lot about your mother.' I think I get it from her – me flamboyance, that is."

"That was when I was young and happy", says Mrs Henry, "and before I had you. You going to have to find yourself a real nice girl with plenty brains, ain't no mistake about that." Mrs Henry, having given as good as she got, goes to put the kettle on. "I'm not a great lover of West Indian food," says Lenny. "But it's all you get here. Sort of brown rice with everything, and chicken on Sundays."

Around their sitting room is a gallery of family photographs, framed and formal. Lenny has three brothers and three sisters. The oldest is more than 30, the youngest 8. "A well-planned 'Dad-had-hiccups' family," says Lenny ironically. In pride of place is an ornately designed message for the whole family: "Christ is the head of this house, the unseen guest at every meal and the silent listener to every conversation."

"That's B.J.", Lenny continues, pointing to a large, gilt-framed reproduction. B.J.? "Black Jesus", he says. "And that's him walking through a field of corn with the lads. Do you know the joke about the messenger who comes to tell all the religious heads of the world what God's like? The first thing he says is: 'She's black'." Ouch! That's a joke? Have you noticed how serious jokes are getting these days? Full of social comment, while straight drama is getting funnier and funnier. "I like really weird jokes, completely undisciplined, disruptive comedy. I adapt stuff from *Mad* magazine, which is brilliant, from cartoons, and I read a lot of American comics. They give me ideas for situations.

"What I like about *The Fosters* is there's no preaching between white and black people. It's not maudlin or heavy. Norman Beaton, though – my father in the show – is a bit of a heavy about the black situation. Keeps telling me how I've got to be the first black this and the first black that. He knows I think he's great – and mental. I'm serious about nothing." Carrot-haired Kay, Lenny's 21 year-old sister, comes in with the tea on a tray just as he's saying how there used to be a picture of him on the wall – as a baby, naked with a big Afro hairstyle, and how he is 'Casanova of the Caribbean', when Kay interrupts. "How does such a big boy get such a little head?" she says. "I kick him when he gets out of hand." And she promptly does. "He's just a 30-bob version of the Six Million Dollar Man," she adds as a last thrust. Justin, Kay's three-year-old son, comes in. "Go play in the traffic, Justin," says Lenny.

Mr Henry senior, a retired factory worker and the odd-man-out in this family which has a quip for everything, pokes his head round the door. He is a small, self-effacing man, pleased at his son's success but wanting none of it himself. "'Ullo dad! Going for a game of darts and a bevy, are yer then, Dad?" Mr Henry removes Justin, who has come back for a slice of the action. He closes the door on his son without having spoken a word, and at the same time shuts out the hurly-burly – pop music, television, the clatter of crocks and pans and Justin's crying – which comes from the rest of the house. "I wish they'd send the scriptwriters of *The Fosters* up here. It's hilarious," says Lenny, and falls

36

The Fosters.
Photo courtesy
of London
Weekend
Television

No preaching between white and black people

uncharacteristically silent for a moment – listening. "It's me Mum having an argument with the telly. She does that, especially when Kojak's on."

The last 18 months have been a heady success story for impressionist and comedian Lenny Henry. First, he went on stage at the London Palladium as a *New Faces* all-time winner, voted 10 out of 10 for star quality by Tony Hatch. Dickie Leeman, producer of *The Golden Shot*, booked him and comedian Charlie Williams asked Lenny to join him in cabaret. He then did a club tour – Batley, Luton, Cardiff and Manchester. After that a show called the royal superstars, before Princess Anne and Captain Mark Phillips, and from October to March he toured and did a winter season with *The Black and White Minstrels*. Straight after *The Fosters*, he is off to the Opera house, Blackpool, for a 16-week summer season. "I've been thrown in the deep end," he says, "where the big money is, but money burns a hole in my pocket. When I need it, it's not there. Sometimes my motor runs so fast even I don't know quite what I'm talking about. I've got to learn to pace myself." Stuart Allen, the producer and director of *The Fosters*, says he's going to strap two 200lb. weights to Lenny's feet and then ask him to move two inches.

The best days of his life, says Lenny, were spent at school. The worst – three months as an £18-a-week engineering apprentice. He says he owes all his success to a certain Alison Keeling. "A classmate," he says. "When the music master asked if anyone could sing, she pushed me up on stage. I stood there with me begging bowl and loin cloth, and instead of singing 'Swing Low Sweet Chariot', I sang 'Jailhouse Rock'. At 8 I wanted to be a boxer, at 11 a fireman and at 13 a rock 'n' roll star. And then, when I was 15, we all used to go to the disco at the Queen Mary Ballroom near Dudley Castle. She pushed me up on stage again there. Somehow, after that, I couldn't keep off stage."

Lenny misses those classmates. They supplied him with gags and helped him write his first four-minute act for *New Faces*. "I had an exercise book full of jokes," he says ruefully, "But somebody has pinched it. When I left school, it was like a well running dry. My source of jokes was gone. I'd like to have time to go round the factories and say 'Well, lads, got any gags?'" As he leaves home to return to London and rehearsals for *The Fosters* (he's contracted to work seven days a week) he yells out in the street to his mother on the doorstep. This time, though, he relents. "Hey Mum! Yer look smashing."

Valerie Clarke, *TV Times*, 10–16 April 1976

NO PROBLEM!

Like most successful British sitcoms it's a comedy based round character rather than slapstick action. The basic situation is simplicity itself. The Powell parents have sold their family business and returned to Jamaica leaving behind their three daughters and two sons in their Willesden semi. Only problem is most of the kids are a touch scatty. Tosh is running a pirate radio station from his upstairs room, while brother Bellamy has rejected people in favour of animals and now lives with his menagerie in a tent in the back garden. Meanwhile, sister Angel has an uphill battle on her hands, trying to run the house and get the bills paid.

The project originated some years ago, when LWT Head of Comedy, Humphrey Barclay, saw the Black Theatre Co-operative in Matura's *Welcome Home, Jacko*. In the summer of 1981, he invited them as a team to prepare a proposal for a comedy series. Last June, the Black Theatre Co-operative held a month-long workshop (paid for by LWT) out of which they devised the format, characters, even some of the storylines. During that time, they also tried to analyse the success of shows such as *Steptoe and Son* and *Fawlty Towers*. So it's perhaps no accident that the series falls squarely into that very English tradition that extols and makes comic the trait of eccentricity. But though comedy in that vein can be soft and fantastical, it also tends to the whimsical and soft.

Certainly, *No Problem!* will probably surprise more than a few fans of the Black Theatre Co-operative. There's little, if any discussion or analysis of the problems facing Britain's black youth. "We felt that if we'd gone 'political', we would have got a slot to match," explains Charlie Hanson, adding that social issues will be forming the basis of the storylines later on in the series. "We want to set its popularity first and then deal with the social issues when everyone is hooked on the characters. And, hopefully hooked on the series."

TV Times, 1–7 January 1983

NO PROBLEM?

Part of Channel 4's strategy has been to build up a black viewing slot on Friday nights. The mid-evening space was first occupied by the appalling reggae documentary *Deep Roots Music*, then by video fragments of performances from the 'Sunsplash' reggae festival for tourists in Jamaica. The latter was used as a curtain-raiser for the comedy series *No Problem!*. If popularity in the black community provides the criterion, then this is probably the most successful of Channel 4's black shows, though it would be wrong to infer too much from this, as passing straws are popular with people who are drowning. This series, which is claimed as a major innovation, parades all the classic attributes of TV sitcom in black form. Its problems arise where the preoccupations of sitcom dovetail with the ideologies of contemporary racism. It must be criticised not only for what it invites white viewers to find funny, but also for the ways in which it represents the black community to itself. These different readings are made possible by the fact that this series, even more effectively than *Black On Black*, transmits the sense of a shared, exclusive culture. The sitcom form, however, allows the excluded to maintain some contact with the show and to laugh at different things, which a common-sense racist perspective identifies as realistic traits of black life. Racist meanings or explanations can therefore be cemented by the series even though it is read by the black audience in a non-realist way.

No Problem! depicts the lives of the five Powell children and their various friends and neighbours after their parents have left Britain and returned to Jamaica, thus structuring the possibility of voluntary repatriation at the heart of the situation. The family is a key site of sitcom, providing an open-ended domestic context which allows the narrative of each episode to be resolved without being closed. Here this familial feeling is expanded to encompass the black audience, who are included by virtue of their familiarity with distinctive norms of black humour and language. But representations of the black family are also at the centre of the racist pathology described above. The absence of the parents means that *No Problem!* presents the black family *a priori* incomplete and deficient. The principal characters also reiterate the racist pathology in a variety of ways. Power relations in the household have been reorganised to compensate for the missing authority of mum and dad. Janet Kay's 'Angel' is the surrogate mother. She runs the house, provides the meals and most of the in-house action takes place in her kitchen.

Her sisters, Shope Shodiende's 'Terri' and Judith Jacob's 'Sensi', represent two views of black female sexuality which contrast with Angel's asexual, matronly, service role. Both are a considerable distance from the conventions of acceptable feminity and racist pathology has endowed each with connotations of deviancy.

Sensi, the tomboy, is masculinised, while Terri, a model by profession, is overt and excessive in her sexuality and the principal vehicle for sexual innuendo in the programme. It is interesting that sexuality is a fundamental aspect of ethnic difference and this allows a much higher level of humour based in sexual themes than would be acceptable in a comparable white sitcom.

Transmits the sense of a shared, exclusive culture

The boys in the programme also fit the pathology framework. Chris Tummings' 'Toshiba' fulfills the older racist stereotype of the clown as well as suggesting that young black men have nothing to offer but machismo, music and wise cracks. His word play and rhyming do, however, offer the black viewer a real source of pleasure. Terri's boyfriend, 'The Beast' (Malcolm Fredrick), is an archetype of criminality – a shady club owner, fashion magnate and businessman eternally on the edge of the big deal. Victor Romero Evans as the animal-loving 'Bellamy' requires separate consideration, since his character is as separate from the stereotypes as the tent he lives in is from the house the rest of his family occupy. Evans is the same actor who portrays 'Moves' in *Black On Black*. As an established actor and singer in his own right, he has built a personal following which savours his performances regardless of the character he is acting out. He and the family's cousin 'Melba' provide the few moments in which comic acting rather than comic situations dominate the show.

Unfortunately, Melba remains a prisoner of the pathology model in that the humour surrounding her based on the generational conflict which is an integral component of the racist account of black family life. Terri describes her age as '25 going on 308' and in the family disagreements she sides with Angel, the residual parent figure.

I am not suggesting that the stereotypes and family orientation of the programme mean that it is readily transferable to reality. For the black audience at least, much of its comedy derives precisely from its distance from the real. Yet the images it offers are as important for what they exclude as for what they present, and the programme rarely fails to block out the idea that there is more to blackness than various combinations of frivolity, religion and sex. *No Problem!* does not refer to or align itself with existing struggles in the black community. In this it perpetuates the idea that blacks themselves, rather than racism, must be the source of all ethnic humour, despite the important start made by Evans and Dhondy (who also co-writes this programme with Mustapha Matura) in challenging this idea via Moves' raps on *Black On Black*.

Where black life fails to generate laughs, the humour of *No Problem!* is created from all the traditional devices of sitcom: mistaken identity, double entendre, unexpected visitors, domestic crises, men dressing as women, and the family simply being stuck with each other. The situations are no more real than the comic personalities which, though scarcely more than vehicles for amusing dialogue, allow the actors to mobilise stereotypes without creating characters. Blacks in particular may laugh at the introduction of a black policeman or magistrate into the lives of the Powells, but this move suggests that the cloak of ethnicity and belongingness is being drawn around them also. The implication that these figures, regardless of their class and role within state institutions, can be a part of one happy black family without any problems cuts right across the direction of comtemporary black politics.

It is tempting to explain the absence of overt politics from the show by arguing that its writers, both well acquainted with the political configuration of the black communities, are probably reluctant to trivialise the political realities involved. This position would obscure the extent to which *No Problem* deals with political issues linked with its authors' previous works. The theme of political organisation has repeatedly been trivialised in a manner which would have done justice to *Citizen Smith*, particularly in the episode (25 February 1983) when two different campaigns with the same initials get muddled up only to unite in a bid to free the 'Willesden One'; and in the show (11 March 1983) when a coup in Beast's home island forms the backdrop to the action. This episode also featured the occupation of Willesden Green against Cruise missiles. *No Problem!* continues the anti-Rasta themes in co-author Mustapha Matura's previous plays, firstly by defining Rasta emphatically outside the family and secondly by making it visible in the ridiculous form of Isaiah, the youth worker from the club down the road. Finally, the authors, who are both of Asian 'ethnic origin', confirm their mastery of the characteristics of Caribbean humour by locking 'West Indian ethnicity' in place with a series of jokes at the expense of the Asian communities which would not be out of place on *Mind Your Language*. A hoard of gags about 'illegal immigrants from Finchley' and 'Abdul the camel driver' are deployed to mark the boundaries of the definition of blackness which is on display. These make it clear that the writers are prepared to sacrifice the fragile nature of political unity between the communities in the name of a laugh.

Paul Gilroy, 'C4 Bridgehead or Bantustan?', *Screen*, July-October 1983

43

*No Problem.
Photo courtesy
of London
Weekend
Television*

Extols and makes comic the trait of eccentricity

OPINION – BRIXTON BLACK WOMEN'S GROUP

The media's image of black women has always misrepresented them. The TV comedy series *No Problem!* is, says the Brixton Black Women's Group no exception. . . With slight variations the images in the mainstream media which have plagued black women fall into four broad categories – 'mammy', matriarch, whore and bitch. These are supposed to represent the sum total of our characteristics.

Even a cursory reading of most literature (with the important exception of what black women write about themselves), reveals limited and distorted views of us; the same holds true for film and television. The reasons for this situation would themselves provide the basis for a fuller examination. But suffice it to say that their existence serves to perpetuate racist and sexist myths about black women, which in the long run amounts to another attempt to undermine black culture generally.

Where efforts are made to deal with us, these are often half-hearted or way off the mark. One of the latest attempts to bring the black face to television – the television series *No Problem!* –

purports to be a show about 'real' black people, but constantly falls back on all the old stereotypes for its humour. Nowhere is this more apparent than in its treatment of black women. The female characters run that limited gauntlet from the scatterbrained 'glamour girl', to the so-called liberated woman who rides a motorbike and puts down the men in the family for not doing an 'honest days work'; to the shrewish 'mother' figure.

Considering the credentials, it is inexcusable that this show gets its laughs at the expense of black people generally, and black women, in particular, because it reinforces long held, erroneous views about who black women are and what we are about. It opts for the easy way out and having done so, is not only unfunny, but blatantly offensive.

For a long time, however, the black woman was (and to a large extent still is) a non-entity as far as the white media is concerned. Her thoughts, feelings, ideas were not ever considered, let alone written about or portrayed. When we finally were 'discovered', it was first as 'mammy' – big-breasted, big eyed, smiling and capable. This Aunt Jemima who was always there performing all the menial, back-breaking work for the 'Miss Anns' for little or no wages, was fostered and became the prominent image of the black woman in the United States from slavery onwards. She was also breeder, which ensured a ready slave supply; although this role was not highlighted by the image makers. . .

City Limits no 126, 2–8 March 1984

THE FRONT LINE

We're sitting in one of Radio London's studios. Alan Igbon, medium height, long, feminine eyelashes, is rolling a rather large cigarette. Paul Barber, wearing a black beret and a seemingly fixed truculent expression, scrutinises the studio's paraphernalia. "Reminds me", says Paul absent-mindedly, "I've got to sign-on on Monday".

They had never met before the audition for *The Front Line*. But they'd heard of each other, even acted in different episodes of the same series – *Boys From The Blackstuff* – and had often been mistaken for each other. Now there's an uncanny closeness between them, as though their roles as brothers in the new sitcom has carried over into real life.

"When we came to read the script", says Paul in a slow, deliberate manner, "we just clicked together.

"The producer gave us a kitchen scene. We argued and kinda got at each other's throats. But at the same time it wasn't heavy. It was brotherly fighting, like families do."

"You gotta give the producer, Roger Race, some credit", interjects Alan, barely looking up from his task. "He recognised it straight-away. So we were given a lot of leeway as to how we were going to play the parts."

In *The Front Line*, a sitcom series filmed in Bristol and Cardiff, they play brothers who live different lifestyles. Sheldon (Alan Igbon) is a Rasta who's forever trying to land his elder and more responsible brother Malcolm (Paul Barber) into trouble. Sheldon regards Malcolm, a security officer with ambitions to join the police, as a sell-out. To make matters worse, Malcolm patrols the front line where Sheldon hangs out.

Like many successful sitcom series, *The Front Line* exploits the lovable rogue figure, in this case Sheldon, and the tension and conflict – and their resolution – within the family. Despite their totally different lifestyles, the two brothers share the same house and remain, despite their arguments, inseparably brothers.

In real life the two actors have a lot in common. They're both from the north – Paul, Liverpool, Alan, Manchester. They're both of West African and British parentage. And they both have first-hand experience of the real front line.

"A front line" explains Paul, "is a place where a lot of black people hang out. It's very communal. Everybody is together. If anything's going to happen on the front line, it's going to be the people there against the police or outsiders. You gotta defend your front line."

According to Paul and Alan, Alex Shearer, the writer, must have put a lot of work into researching the series. He actually lives close to the St Paul's area of Bristol, which figured in the 1981 riots.

Alex, says Paul, was very receptive to suggestions based on their own experiences. "He kept close to us. We were able to talk to Alex and tell him that we've had this or that experience and found it funny at the time, and he'd go and write it down and make it funny as well."

Despite the series' setting and characters, they're convinced that it will go down well with both black and white audiences, with the possible exception of Rastas. "I don't think" says Alan, "that they are going to take lightly the levity of the show, depicting a Rasta as a comical figure. Your hardline Rastas might be a bit uptight, annoyed. . . ."

"I don't think they will", Paul interjects. "It might be fun for them to watch everyday situations on the front line, like the handshakes that take half-an-hour, and the way people talk."

"But it's not a black show", Alan emphasises. "We're two black boys from up north, and people all over England are going to recognise the accents. With Sheldon, when he's feeling militant and rootsy, he'll go into the Jamaican accent. But when he's drinking or eating with his brother they talk normal."

"And that's what happens in real life", says Paul, in a thick Liverpudlian accent which eight years of living in London hasn't erased. "Black people switch from one accent to another depending on who they're talking to. . . .". Alan comes in again: "We're black British people. We're not ashamed of it, we're not proud of it. That's just what we are."

Paul nods in agreement: "The script gave us the opportunity to say things that I think the majority of black people born in England will feel and want to say. This gives us the opportunity to voice it for them in a comical way. . ."

Alan again: "The series portrays black people not just as black people but as human beings, and that's something white audiences will be able to pick up on immediately. They'll say: 'Oh, yeah, I do that or I say that to my brother or my brother says that to me'."

"It's making some serious points as well", says Paul, "but in a funny way. Like there's a scene when Sheldon goes to complain to a shop-keeper about the skin-coloured plasters which don't match his skin colour. The shopkeeper says: 'It's your fault, you

The Frontline.
Photo courtesy
of BBC

Everyday situations on the frontline

got the wrong colour skin.' As if it's only white people who cut themselves. Fabulous points, you know. You laugh at them because the scenes are funny, the way Sheldon's trying to protest, but it also makes you sit back and think: yes, it's true, it's positively true."

Both actors enthuse over their involvement in the series. Alan feels that it gives him a better chance to express himself than any other television show he has done in the past. "*The Front Line* allows me to get relevant messages across to the public. If it can say something to integrate and break down ignorant barriers between people, it'll be a good thing." For Paul, their performances in *The Front Line* augur well for other black actors. "The series shows that you can get one or two black actors and they can really make a thing gel, and we can really work just as well as white actors, given the opportunity. We can make a plot work. We can make people laugh. We can make people think."

There have, of course, been other predominantly black comedy shows on British television before. But they've been shortlived. Alan believes that this series will be more successful than others, because it is a result of a tight working relationship between producer, writer and actors. "It's got a lot of soul, man," he says passionately. They clearly enjoyed making the series, but their eyes are already on the future. Alan has just finished filming in St Lucia with Michael Caine. And Paul has just completed a two-hander for an independent production company.

But much of their future work will depend on the success of *The Front Line*. "If it's a success", says Alan, "it should give us the opportunity to exercise more choice in our work. We will be able to say about a script: 'I don't believe in the writer's words – I can work myself into the ground, but I can't make this work' that's one aspect." As for Paul, he'd be contented if the series just helps to show that black people are human beings. . . "to break down some of the stereotypes. . . show that we laugh and cry at the same things. . . . And, it might mean I wouldn't be in the dole office too much."

Ferdi Dennis, *Radio Times*, 1–7 December 1984

TANDOORI NIGHTS

CURRY ON LAUGHING

They thought of calling it *Chapatti's Over*. They tried *Tandoori is the Night*, and even toyed with *Paperback Raita*. Eventually, Channel Four settled on *Tandoori Nights* for their new situation comedy beginning this Thursday. Saeed Jaffrey (whose grandfather, back in the days of the Raj, was Prime Minister of the state of Maler Kotla) plays Jimmy Sharma, the proprietor of an elegant curry house called 'The Jewel in the Crown'. Immediately opposite, one of his waiters launches a rival establishment, 'The Far Pavillion'.

Tandoori Nights. Photo courtesy of Channel 4

An equal opportunities offender?

The situation affects us all. As Jimmy says, "Apart from the Kama Sutra, the Indian restaurant is the most celebrated export of the Indian subcontinent. . ."

TV Times, 29 June–5 July 1985

If you are not Asian, but aware of the purposeful way Channel 4 goes about catering for ethnic groups, you are likely to approach this affair with a certain reserve. Are the Indians about to degrade themselves to curry favour? On the evidence of two episodes it is hard to judge what they are aiming for. But this is partly because of the culturally unemphatic world the British Indian – unlike the British West Indian – inhabits.

In the opening episode, the owner of 'The Jewel in the Crown' restaurant, deserted by his waiter, tries to give his eaterie a bit of class by hiring a wine waiter, and so outclass his rival, 'The Far Pavillion'. This introduces the expected inverted discrimination joke: an aspiring white waiter is ushered out with the words, "The Indian rope-trick cannot be done by a Chinaman". The staff solemnly advise that racialism must be combatted: "You've got to start somewhere." An incompetent old Indian has already offered his services, humbly: "I am a monkey, you are the organ-grinder, boss." But the boss, an entrepreneurial 'socialist' stifles his principles (of which the script gives no evidence) and hires a young man whose only motive is to get to know his younger daughter, Asha.

Meanwhile, look whom Dad has coming to dinner! A white lady (Angela Browne), whom he met on a golf course. Asha is peeved. "Because she is white!" accuses her elder sister, Bubbly (Shelley King), a socially responsible lady who works in an Asian Advice Centre. But the lady is so boringly 'into' things Indian – obliging the family to eat with their fingers out of politeness, that Dad goes off her. With a couple of reinforcements – a scheming cook; a grandmother, who plays the ponies – that's the set-up.

It is interesting to apply without vehemence – since the series' writer, Farrukh Dhondy, says, rightly, that one shouldn't try to make a soapbox out of comedy – the criticisms one would expect to direct at a white man's play which 'flirted' with inter-racial romance. The solution here is a cop-out. Before the romance can go any distance, or any description of the relationship is attempted, the white woman is discarded only because she is tedious. So the racial issue is raised and sidestepped in good old Hollywood style (hardly any touching).

While the subsidiary characters, such as the chef, and later, a film star's agent, tend to be stereotypes of sly wheeler-dealers, some of the characters are pathetic racial types which could recall the Stepin Fetchits of early Hollywood. The old monkey-to-the-organ-grinder man is pathetic: unskilled, childishly servile. But we don't know yet whether Mr Dhondy has unwittingly lapsed into a kind of racialism because servility is, of course, appropriate to the context. We are in a world of masters and waiters, (none of them, alas, as dizzily funny as Basil Fawlty's).

It may be as much a tribute to the degree that Indians have been assimilated by British society (not necessarily a good thing) as a criticism of the writing that we do not have a powerful sense of watching an ethnic comedy. If the characters were Red Indians, store or reservation, their cultural dilemma would provide more original material. The Scots are more 'foreign' than the family at 'Jewel in the Crown'.

Tandoori Nights. Photo courtesy of Channel 4

A comedy, not a soapbox

In a later episode, we have the younger daughter being a starry-eyed fan of an Indian film star who is brought to the restaurant for a publicity stunt. (The weakness of this episode is that the daughter, Rita Wolf, is a young actress of such restless verve and transparent shrewdness that you don't believe for a minute she would go soppy about anyone. The tete-a-tete suggests equality, with the girl winning on self-possession points.) The fact that the daughter prefers videos or Indian films, and is briefly stuck on an Indian film star does not in itself create an 'Indian' situation, since the characters do not do or say anything which would differ from what white British people would do or say, and there is no evidence of any distinct cultural force at work guiding them.

But there is one distinction: the Britishness of these Indians is anachronistic (aside from a passing reference to a porno video). These characters exist in the world of *Brief Encounter*. They may be romantic, but so far they are asexual. And it is wonderful to watch a situation comedy and know you are not likely (I hope) to be bludgeoned by references to knickers and boobs. The humour is gentle, and a kind of mildness pervades the stories. The actors perform with a will, with the very serviceable Saeed Jaffrey very much in command.

Peter Lennon, *The Listener*, 27 June 1985

T*andoori Nights* (Channel 4) is likewise an equal opportunities offender. It's a promising sitcom about an up-market curry house called 'The Jewel in the Crown', owned by one Jimmy Sharma (Saeed Jaffrey), an upwardly mobile Indian proprietor. Episode 1 established Jimmy's credentials as a grasping, unscrupulous greasy and successful capitalist who aspires not only to wealth, but social acceptability (i.e. white women) as well. His ambitions in these regards, however, are threatened by various things. Two doors away, his Bangladeshi ex-waiter has opened a rival establishment called, originally enough, 'The Far Pavillion'. And Jimmy's two daughters turn out to be both sexy and left-wing, which is not at all what Indian girls should be.

What's interesting about *Tandoori Nights* is not that it's wryly funny (which it is), or that it's slickly produced, but that it somehow seems able to get away with poking fun at subjects which are normally considered out of bounds in civilised society. For example, Jimmy's throw-away contempt for his ex-employee turned rival is expressed in generalisations about the traditional lack of hygiene of citizens of Bangladesh. This is the kind of thing which would land the rest of us in court for incitement to racial hatred, or at least earn us a punch on the nose for sheer offensiveness. But in *Tandoori Nights* it just comes across as the kind of thing one restaurateur might say of another. Most mysterious.

John Naughton, *The Listener*, 11 July 1985

THE LENNY HENRY SHOW

WRITERS? THEY'RE CRUCIAL!

Is it difficult for two white writers to create convincing black comedy? Cambridge graduates Stan Hey and Andrew Nickolds – the men behind the laughs for the enormously successful *Lenny Henry Show* – get fed up being asked that question.

"Race", says Stan emphatically, "isn't an issue. What we're writing about are working people. There are a lot of similarities between Lenny's and our backgrounds.

"Good comedy needs recognisable characters. Delbert Wilkins is a larger-than-life character. The setting is believable. There are kids like that from all races. They fancy themselves, and they're always breaking their mother's hearts."

"We explore aspects of Delbert's life", says Andrew. "It doesn't matter that we're not black. We don't deliberately write black. Lenny interprets our script, using the street talk and things like that."

"Delbert", says Lenny Henry, "is this crucial dresser and there's a part of him that's in all of us. A slightly childish, irresponsible attitude. But Winston (Vas Blackwood) is there to look after him."

Lenny explains that a lot of the material is generated by him. His family and friends in Birmingham – where he was born – and London provide models or incidents for the shows. This is, undoubtedly, part of the show's secret. Much of the humour and situations rings true. In the new series, for instance, Lenny's girlfriend becomes pregnant and he's torn between flight and facing up to his responsibilities.

The emphasis on developing and exploring different aspects of the character, Stan believes, distinguishes *The Lenny Henry Show* from those now infamous racial comedies of the 1970s. "They were prehistoric", says Stan. "Some of the jokes now sound quite offensive."

The duo, who have written together for 15 years, met at Cambridge, where they discovered a shared passion for *Bilko*. They started by writing for several series, including ITV's *Hazel* and *Agony*, and in 1985 BBC1's *Hold the Back Page!*

Stan Hey's BBC *Screen Two* film *Coast to Coast* – which gave Lenny Henry his first serious role – was the meeting point for Lenny, Stan and Andrew. Its storyline and setting were derived from Stan's experiences of frequenting black nightclubs in Liverpool as a teenager.

Another film project in the pipeline is taken from Lenny's uncle's experience of coming to Britain on the *Empire Windrush*. That and many other projects suggest the new series might be the last for a while. "Lenny could go on to anything", says Stan. "He could be bigger than Eddie Murphy."

Ferdi Dennis, *Radio Times*, 10–16 September 1988

THE CRUCIAL ART OF AIR PIRACY

Delbert Wilkins, who has hovered so long on the edge of his 30th birthday, is in grave danger of surrendering to maturity. That is why the fifth series of *The Lenny Henry Show*, six half-hour shows starting tonight, is likely to be the last in this form. In this ageist era it is apparently inconceivable that such idealism as Delbert manifests, can last over 29 years.

While his peers give in to legitimate broadcasting, Delbert clings to the idea of radio air piracy as purity. While others search for commercial success, with whatever is conventional and bland, he maintains his fresh faced integrity and his nil ratings. As far as can be seen he talks to the microphone and himself.

Aficionados will remember that Delbert has lost control of the BBC, otherwise the Brixton Broadcasting Company. Alex, the

*The Lenny
Henry Show.
Photo courtesy
of BBC*

Race not an issue

unspeakable new boss, has obtained a licence for the erstwhile
pirate station and made it look suspiciously new painted.

As if this was not bad enough he has employed the defrocked
PC Lillie to give advice to listeners, and the devoted Winston
(Vas Blackwood) as the star deejay, the housewife's choice. If the
BBC is amused and silenced during the six weeks that would be
no more than it deserved.

For his part Delbert, with Winston and girlfriend Claudette
(Nimmy Marsh) soon in tow again, retaliates with Crucial FM. The
new pirate station is set up in the penthouse flat of a decrepit
south London tower block. The electricity is unreliable and so are
the programmes but a presence has been re-established.

"Your're listening to Crucial FM, the station with total access
. . . paid for by credit, playing plastic and keeping flexible hours.

And I'm going to open my account with a highly appropriate record ... Odyssey and 'Back To My Roots'", Delbert tells anybody who may by some miracle be listening.

Not that Lenny Henry, originally a Black Country comedian and still sporting the accent of the English West Midlands, makes anything of his parents' West Indian roots. His script writers understand that race is not a primary issue for him, rather he wants to raise matters of general working-class concern.

In this latest opener, 'Back To My Roots', Stan Hey and Andrew Nickolds have concentrated on routes to a new start and a better life. The dress may be garish and the manner childish but there is no attempt at escapism. Delbert fancies himself but his judgement of others is as sharp as his new haircut.

Invited to talk about the general level of television sitcom just now, Henry is withering in his scorn. He sees most of it as entirely blinkered in its preconception, reflecting a suburban and middle-class culture, akin to sticking your head in a laurel bush.

Every now and then Delbert's words are wise and aware but I guess this is to a large extent incidental to Lenny's popularity. The truth is that his charm is not so much in what he says as the way that he says it. He has a likeable personality, much skill in timing and is one of the funniest men around.

Sean Day-Lewis, *The Scotsman*, 15 September 1988

CREDITS AND TRANSMISSION DATES

TILL DEATH US DO PART

Written by: Johnny Speight
Producer: Dennis Main Wilson
Music by: Dennis Wilson
Production Company: BBC
Tx dates: 1966–1974

CAST
Warren Mitchell (Alf); Dandy Nichols (Else); Anthony Booth (Mike); Una Stubbs (Rita).

LOVE THY NEIGHBOUR

Written by: Vince Powell & Harry Driver
Producer: Stuart Allen
Production Company: Thames Television
Tx dates: 1972–1975

CAST
Jack Smethurst (Eddie Booth); Kate Williams (Joan Booth); Rudolph Walker (Bill Reynolds); Nina Baden-Semper (Barbara Reynolds)

THE FOSTERS

Written by: John Donley & Kurt Taylor
Producer: Stuart Allen
Production Company: London Weekend Television
Tx dates: 9.4.76–2.7.76 (1st series)
16.4.77–9.7.77 (2nd series)

CAST
Sharon Rosita (Shirley Foster); Lenny Henry (Sonny Foster); Isabelle Lucas (Pearl Foster); Norman Beaton (Samuel Foster); Lawrie Mark (Benjamin Foster); Carmen Munro (Vilma)

NO PROBLEM!

Written by: Farrukh Dhondy & Mustapha Matura
Producer: Charlie Hanson
Production Company: London Weekend Television
Tx dates: 7.1.83–11.3.83 (1st series)
14.1.84–31.3.84 (2nd series)
27.4.85–1.6.85 (3rd series)

CAST
Victor Romero Evans (Bellamy); Judith Jacob (Sensimilia); Janet Kay (Angel); Shope Shodeinde (Terri); Chris Tummings (Toshiba); Malcolm Frederick ('the Beast')

THE FRONT LINE

Written by: Alex Shearer
Producer: Roger Race
Music and lyrics by: Black Roots
Production Company: BBC
Tx dates: 6.12.84–17.1.85

CAST
Paul Barber (Malcom); Alan Igbon (Sheldon); Ronny Cush (Earl); Julie Brennon (Maria); Jenni George (Lousie); Shaun Curry (Inspector)

TANDOORI NIGHTS

Series devised by: Farrukh Dhondy
Producer: Malcolm Craddock
Production Company: Picture Palace for Channel 4
Tx dates: 4.7.85–8.8.85 (1st series)
9.10.87–13.11.87 (2nd series)

CAST
Saeed Jaffrey (Jimmy); Zohra Segal (Gran); Rita Wolf (Asha); Shelley King (Bubbly); Tariq Unus (Alaudin); Badi Uzzaman (Rashid); Andrew Johnson (Noor)

THE LENNY HENRY SHOW

Written by: Stan Hey & Andrew Nickolds
Producer: Geoff Posner
Production Company: BBC
Tx dates: 27.10.87–1.12.87 (1st series in sitcom format)
15.09.88–3.11.88 (2nd series)

CAST
Lenny Henry (Delbert Wilkins); Vas Blackwood (Winston); Michael Mears (Alex); Gina McKee (Julie); Naim Khan (Wazim); Malcolm Rennie (Lillie); Nimmy March (Claudette)

PART TWO

I FOUGHT THE LAW

Drama Series and Serials

INTRODUCTION
Jim Pines

In her discussion of *Widows*, Charlotte Brunsdon comments on how "the crime series offers particular problems for the representation of race if the production company wishes to move away from the stereotypical presentation of black villains. The problem" she adds, "lies in the way in which the effect of realism is created in a genre."[1] According to genre theory, this 'reality effect' has more to do with the reality constructed in other crime series than with the 'real world' or social reality as such. Analytic stress is therefore placed on the aesthetic (iconographic) elements which define the crime genre – i.e. its internal dynamic, its 'recognisable repertoire of conventions' – thus discouraging reductionist 'realist' (or sociological) readings of the genre's tendencies.[2] In relation to black representation, this critical framework would seem to suggest that it is primarily the generic codes and conventions which work against the construction of black characterisation outside the familiar patterns of racial stereotyping, rather than anything specifically to do with 'race relations' discourses. If that is the case, then the obvious question pops up: is the crime genre inherently racist?

A number of crime dramas consciously set out to create 'positive' black characters, although these characters usually appear against a preponderance of 'negative' villainous types in the narratives. This is particularly evident in *Wolcott*, where the construction of the eponymous black cop figure as 'hero' (an image which many black viewers would regard as a blatant contradiction in terms) depends almost entirely on the criminal-isation of 'the black community' (cf. the Pakistani hero, Ahmed

Khalil, in *Gangsters*). Imruh Caesar et al. are correct in stressing this point about *Wolcott* and particularly the 'Americanisation' of the black British ghetto milieu.[3] Indeed, the serial has all the trappings of a seventies Hollywood 'blaxploitation' cop film, which happens to be set in Britain and which deploys only a small number of elements of the detective genre. This makes it a good example of the kind of slippage that often occurs when black characters and situations are the centre of narrative attention in genre films or TV drama. The 'realism' invoked in such drama of the black criminal milieu, relies heavily on popular racist imagery of 'black crime' which is represented in an unquestioned manner for dramatic effect. This construction not only undermines whatever liberal intentions the film or TV drama might have had, but it also tends to identify the narrative as a populist (and often reactionary) form of 'race relations' drama.

In some respects, *The Bill* conforms to this pattern of racial representation, particularly in episodes which centre on P.C. Haynes and a 'black community' situation. But Haynes' presence has never been a serious point of tension in the series, though his arrival at Sun Hill Station initially provoked the usual (stereotypic) racial references. He has since become an integrated member of the force, with noticeably little direct reference to his 'colour', or rather, to 'race' as a problem issue as such. In a recent episode – 'Duty Elsewhere' (31 January 1989) – he is seconded to Peckham to infiltrate a local black gang. Although his blackness is relevant to the task, it is presented (both to him and to the viewer) as a normal part of his job as a police officer, it is merely a convenient asset. This 'integration' of the Haynes character works within the conventions of the half-hour police series and is structured in such a way as to maintain the overall consistency or identity of *The Bill* (i.e. its recognisable features). This construction also fits in with what Geoffrey Hurd has said about the typical police series which "does not simply reflect the social world of policing but must actively construct a coherent vision of social reality within which the playing out of the nightly drama of law and order can be contained."[4] The representation of the black villains in this episode could also be read as part of the same ideological process, i.e. while they are clearly marked as 'black', they are nonetheless presented as an isolated segment of (black) society which conforms more to typical villainy. It isn't so much that 'race'

Wolcott. Photo courtesy of Thames Television

All the trappings of a seventies Hollywood 'blaxploitation' cop film

is irrelevant in integrationist crime narratives such as these, but more the way in which it is played down or assimilated into the exigencies of the generic conventions. Another good example of how this process operates is *Rockcliffe's Babies*, which is perhaps more significant in terms of gender and the power relations between Rockcliffe and his women detectives.

American films and TV crime series tend to be more sophisticated than their British counterparts in handling racial themes and imagery. Take an early film example, *Odds Against Tomorrow* (1959), which Colin McArthur identified as part of the cycle of gangster films made during the fifties "in which a group of men from various backgrounds. . .come together for the

65

purpose of the robbery, the rewards of which they are kept from enjoying by internal tensions and, sometimes, malicious fate."[5] What is interesting about this film is the way in which the racial element (i.e. the presence of a black member of the gang) represents only one of several tensions which threaten group cohesion, which is integrated into the narrative and works within the conventions of the genre. Of course, 'race relations' is privileged in the story – hence the black-white confrontation at the end of the film – but it does not function as a stereotypic plot device designed simply to elicit exaggerated racial effect (which is often the case with many British crime dramas including *Widows*, where racial badgering provides incidental moments of racist light relief, but otherwise has no ethical value in the narrative).

Generally speaking, these kinds of incidental derogatory scenes which could be said to derive mainly from the sitcom tradition (the primary site of racist humour and mockery in television) are not a common feature in American programmes. 'Race' operates in a much more subtle fashion in US-based (urban) drama and certainly since the seventies, moreover, there is no longer a stigma attached to the representation of black (or ethnic) villains, so there is no need to invoke racist caricature. This is evident in the popular police series *Hill Street Blues*, which not only covers the whole panoply of multi-ethnic urban American society, but at the same time succeeds in 'naturalising' (neutralising?) social and ethnic divisions within the general flow of the narrative.

Although many of the series' dramatic 'situations' centre on some kind of inter-ethnic interaction, they generally are not presented just in those terms (i.e. 'race' does not occupy a privileged space), except, perhaps sporadically, when the story situation involves a threatening riot in the non-white community/ ghetto. Indeed, the series' celebrated 'open' structure enables it to elide moral concerns and to play down 'race relations' issues. What would have been read (say) twenty years ago as 'racial caricature', e.g. some of the ghetto 'types' that come into contact with the precinct, today are read as 'characters' in the quaint sense of the term. Some people might argue that this proves how it is possible to incorporate racial themes and imagery into the TV crime series, without always resorting to more obvious racial or race relations stereotypes.

Hill Street Blues. Photo courtesy of Channel 4

Covers the whole panoply of multi–ethnic urban, American society

However, when you look closely at any number of TV police/crime shows, both British and to a lesser extent American, you find that black characters (and black-related situations) tend to be characterised in quite narrow terms. Typically, villains are linked to drugs, violent street crime (e.g. mugging), and prostitution (a particular favourite with white male writers vis-a-vis the image of black women); while 'heroes', on the other hand, are often characterised as noble figures whose destiny it is to 'clean up the criminalised black neighbourhoods'! You will not find any white collar black villains, corporate gangsters (a la the mafia), or computer-based defrauders in the urban crime drama.

In other words, in sharp contrast to the white police/gangster milieu, which relies on a wide variety of character-types and situations, black-related motifs tend to be circumscribed by a rigid set of popular images already in circulation in (white) society, and this inevitably limits the extent to which black villains and heroes are able to enter into the mainstream of 'the (non) criminal universe'. This is not a problem of the crime genre as such, I would argue, but rather the result of 'race relations' conventions which have permeated all areas of mainstream media/racial representation. The problem is further compounded by the sense in which white writers and producers, by and large, seem incapable of approaching black subjects imaginatively, i.e. beyond the narrow confines of tabloid race imagery. Even a well-crafted series like *London's Burning*, for example, can't resist the final 'race relations' statement: the manner in which the noble black firefighter (Ethnic) is 'killed off' in the play on which the series was based, is a story device employed in many integrationist narratives. 'Good' blacks often become integrated through some form of martyrdom! However, as I've tried to suggest in relation to *The Bill* and *Rock'cliffe's Babies*, British TV crime fiction seems to be moving gradually towards the kind of 'de-racialised' black imagery which we see in some American programmes – though some cynics might argue that this is only a tactical move within the industry, due to the requirements of the American marketplace, where programmes need to be sold, and

London's Burning. Photo courtesy of London Weekend Television

Can't resist the final 'race relations' statement

viewers hold different expectations vis-a-vis images of black people.

Gangsters is widely regarded as an innovative piece of TV (crime) drama. It was certainly the first TV drama to invoke in a highly stylised (and seductive) manner the strange milieu that is often constructed around race-related urban, crime narratives. There is nothing like it elsewhere in either TV documentaries or other kinds of TV drama. It is as if the 'otherness' of the black subject – and its socially marginalised location – have been pushed to extremes both visually and narratively. In that respect, crime fiction is the most intriguing (dare I say it, exciting) form of racial (and racist) imagery in British television – certainly more so than sitcoms and soaps which are fixed in relatively static formulaic conventions and tiresome in their endless regurgitation of old racist jokes and dramatically uninteresting situations. Though the majority of programmes eschew the excesses of (say) *Gangsters*, Farrukh Dhondy's *King of the Ghetto* does show the facility with which the crime genre is able to incorporate 'experimental' or idiosyncratic forms of (racial) representation, notwithstanding the sort of issues raised by Fatima Salaria in her critique of the serial, of course.[6]

The sense of immediacy is obviously an important element in the 'success' of the TV crime fiction – the (racial) topicality of many of its themes and imagery are clearly drawn from what can be best described as 'tabloid reality', which gives the stories their particular energy. TV crime drama often evokes a kind of vulgarity which seems to go straight to the heart of British social anxieties, which other kinds of TV programme (including race relations documentaries) rarely, if ever manage to achieve. However, the question remains whether TV police/crime drama has opened up new possibilities in representing blacks within mainstream generic conventions, or whether it has simply reinforced racist imagery, only now in a strikingly stylish and seductive manner.

I'm inclined towards the latter, not because I think the crime genre is *ipso facto* racist (there is much evidence to show otherwise), but because most writers and producers of these programmes have rarely attempted to incorporate black imagery *within* the conventions of the genre, experimentally or otherwise. This makes it difficult, therefore, to study black-related crime drama, without constant reference to the exigencies of 'race relations' representation. Thus, the temptation for sociological analyses, around, say, the problem of racial stereotypes, often becomes too hard to resist. My own feeling is that most of the drama should be treated as primarily 'race relations' narratives, and then explored for the ways in which they attempt to incorporate certain mainstream generic conventions: i.e. focusing on the tension between the two.

One of the complaints about recent television has been that while blacks are quantitatively more visible (particularly in the US) the quality of their roles still leaves much to be desired. Although the presence of blacks in mainstream drama is often seen as an important break with the sitcom tradition, the conventions (and I mean this in the old-fashioned pejorative sense) used to structure black imagery into the narratives have tended to revert to more popular (and often reactionary) racial and social stereotypes. My argument is that this common tendency should be challenged and its relevance questioned, both critically and industrially (i.e. within production practices). The possibility of more interesting uses of the crime genre should be explored in relation to the wide diversity of black and white experiences, expectations, desires and fantasies.

Notes

(1) Charlotte Brunsdon, 'Men's Genres for Women' in *Boxed In : Women and Television*, eds. Helen Baehr and Gillian Dyer (Pandora 1987) p.192. The section on 'Bella' in *Widows* is reprinted in this collection.
(2) For an overview of genre theories see, *The Cinema Book,* ed. Pam Cook (BFI 1985)
(3) Imruh Caesar, Henry Martin, Colin Prescod, Menelik Shabazz, *Grass Roots*, March 1981, reprinted in this collection.
(4) Geoffrey Hurd, 'The Television Presentation of the Police,' in *Popular Television and Film*, eds. Tony Bennett et al. (BFI/The Open University 1981) p.56
(5) Colin McArthur, *Underworld USA* (Secker & Warburg 1972) p.53
(6) Fatima Salaria, *Artrage*, Issue 17, 1987, reprinted in this collection.

GANGSTERS

GANGSTERS OF BOOM TOWN 1976

The Midlands aren't what they used to be. The 'provincial' tag has lost its drowsy overtone. "Just look at the Birmingham skyline," says David Rose, producer of the new six-part crime serial, *Gangsters*. "Look at the tower blocks, the mixture of races in the streets. There's a difference in the air. It's edgy, electric. We're in Boom Town 1976. That's the feeling of excitement and suspense we want to convey."

He's emphatic that *Gangsters* – which deals with gang-wars, the smuggling of drugs and immigrants and the prostitution racket – is not Birmingham-based. "It's not about one city. It is symptomatic of any big Midlands town." But Birmingham is where the story began. "I invited writer Philip Martin to join the BBC script department at Birmingham where I'd gone to develop regional drama and told him to look around for three months to see if he could find a subject which interested him. He walked the streets and talked to the police and visited the clubs and at the end of it he wrote his play, *Gangsters*. It ended with the death of Rawlinson, a gang-leader and nightclub owner and John Kline, a visiting villain from London, waiting to be charged with his manslaughter. The series, also called *Gangsters*, takes the story from there. Unexpectedly set free, he's approached by Khan, a Pakistani undercover agent working for one of the security services. Kline, he suggests, could help him penetrate the white underworld."

Rose believes in rooting his thrillers in actuality. "Not only in incident. The regions in which they're set also give them a special flavour." He was the founding father of *Z Cars* – set in Lancashire – and ran the programme for four years. *Softly, Softly* transferred the action to Bristol and *Task Force* moved on to the Medway. "One of the jobs of regional drama is to develop new writers and new actors," says Rose. "I also think it's vital to strike up an association with regional theatres. Birmingham Rep, for instance, put on *Trinity Tales*, a play by Alan Plater best-known for his television work, with Bill Maynard and Francis Matthews. And the play was then adapted for television: that kind of contact is helpful to us all."

Gangsters
Photo courtesy
of BBC

A breakthrough in several directions

Gangsters, he thinks, represents a breakthrough in several directions. "It must be the first ever television series to have a Pakistani hero. He's played by Ahmed Khalil. Kline, his reluctant accomplice, is played by Maurice Colbourne. Certainly it's violent and the language is a good deal tougher than you'd have heard on television, say, five years ago. But we're reproducing life. I have to rely on 20 years' experience to judge what is

72

suitable and what isn't. I'm not in business to titillate or offend anyone."

The violence in the series is frequently stylised, he says: "Almost to the point of resembling pop art. It's gaudy and brash, the stuff of entertainment." There's literally a smashing climax to the first episode in which Kline and Khan are trapped in a derelict building by West Indian gangsters who plan to do them in by demolishing the house with a massive steel ball and chain. The ball swings towards the crumbling bolt-hole. The image freezes and the caption rolls 'To be continued next week...' Batman and Robin have rarely found themselves in tighter spots.

At the same time, says Rose, *Gangsters*, with its cast of strippers and punters, rogues and racketeers, has been filmed with a rare feeling for atmosphere. "We've used a hand-held electronic camera which can go wherever an actor can go. It's increased the pace and fluidity enormously." What pleases him most is the veracity of the series. "We make no distinction between races or colours. The heroes and villains are black, brown and white just as you'd expect them to be." Best of all, he adds: "There's hardly a policeman in sight".

Radio Times, 9 September 1976

The Pebble Mill Press Release for the second series announced that: "As the original *Play for Today* of *Gangsters* used the idiom of the gangster movie and the subsequent TV series the style of the Saturday Morning Serial, the second TV series retains a more varied form of the cliffhanger ending – this time reflecting some of the 'Yellow Peril' and 'Fu Manchu' movies of the twenties and thirties as well as referring to the recent wave of 'Kung Fu' films." Rather less sympathetically, in a review of the second series, Richard Last complained that it was like a "...compound of leavings from *The Avengers*, *Monty Python*, early Laurel and Hardy, late Ken Russell, *Who Do You Do?* and *Batman*... with a touch of *The Prisoner* thrown in... You can't get too many laughs from a W.C.Fields impersonation when it is liable to be followed by painful death and wild realistic grief, or relax with jokes like a tombstone inscribed 'Sacred to the Memory of Bryan Cowgill' when a few frames further on an elderly Asian will be beaten up by white hooligans. Mr Martin was trying to play tennis without benefit of net or marker lines and it can't be done. Without rules of any kind credibility perishes."

From an unpublished paper by Paul Kerr, June 1978

The more difficult area in the text is race, because on the surface it appears so central from the play and the multiplicity of racial groups represented. As already outlined the sting in the tail is the complex 'truth' of the mugging incident. However the placing of the other ethnic characters (Rafiq, Kuldip, Sarah Gant, Malleson, Dermot, W.C.Fields) is much harder to trace through the text especially as the complex of codes develops towards its denouement. As Barthes has noted "what stands out, emphasizes and impresses are the semes, the cultural citations and symbols", and there is a sense in which characters act as representatives of racial groups in the play and Series 1, but, as the text progresses, it is the intratextuality that becomes more important than the initial posing. Thus Rafiq after his initial depiction as a community leader acting with great duplicity in his dealings (involvement with Rawlinson, illegal immigration racket, blackmail) magically aids detection of corrupt leaders in the first series, and after initial cooperation with the Triads, magically evades arrest and ends up (with Kuldip) agent of the US Narcotics Bureau, in the second series. The stylisation of camerawork in his house, the jokiness of the scenes, deny the initial trajectory (corrupt community leader) of its force, turning into a comedy of textual acrobatics. Race is significant at the end (in the mugging), but the ethnic multiplicity of the characters becomes of the text, not of society. They act as a part of the pleasures of excess in the text. This contrasts with the force of the character of Dinah in the play, whose powerful dialogue is ended by repatriation (in a coffin) at the same time as the deportation of the illegal immigrant.

In the second series the posing of enigmas become less important, the cultural references obscured, as actions and the symbolic (the supernatural, the telex, the lucid qualities of the signification – through film, subtitling etc.) dominate the text and its pleasurability through multiple internal complexities. The hardness of the original is almost lost to an elaborate see-the-point exercise. Play becomes playful. But wit and comedy are centred in the unconscious as is our scopophilic delight in looking, so that in the end the covering over is thrust aside to distress through a realism (the mugging). "The truth is. . .long desired and avoided, kept in a kind of pregnancy for its full term, a pregnancy whose end, both liberating and catastrophic, will bring about the utter end of the discourse." (Barthes) The end distresses, pains our delight in looking; the excess of the justice/England antithesis saturates the text, but is in turn liberated by Anne's liberation of our look.

The last episodes, the final realisation of the enigmas of the idiosyncratic (if heavily influenced in a realist style) play, heavily centred on issues and Birmingham, through the excess and liberation from the conventional mode into the extremes of a surrealist style, are the expression of an un-institutionalised drama, a regional structure unbound and justified. The final reassertion of the televisual version of 'reality' through the complex appropriation of the signifiers of mugging, foregrounds an absence that brings the voice of the real (the author) back to haunt and depress, as despite Anne's liberating look he is seen dictating the end of the script and throwing it to the wind.

From an unpublished paper by Richard Paterson, June 1978

WOLCOTT

MEET THE FIRST BLACK PRINCE OF THE POLICE

Most American television detective series now star black as well as white actors to reflect a multi-racial society on the screen. Now it has happened in Britain. Shaft and Co. have been joined by Winston Churchill Wolcott, black British sleuth. In an exclusive interview, we talk to actor George William Harris who could become the biggest – and sexiest – detective star of them all.

He's Big. He's Black. In his own unequivocal terms he's a 'classy dude'. The name is Winston Churchill Wolcott, and he is Britain's first black television detective to get a show of his own – our answer to Sidney Poitier's Mr Tibbs in *In the Heat of the Night*. And should you be left in any doubt as to the classy dude's appeal then actor George William Harris, who plays him, is happy to supply you with ample confirmation of it.

"He's a policeman in the greatest essence of the word. I see him coming from a long line of mythical figures out of Scotland Yard. There was Sherlock Holmes. There was Sexton Blake. You can put Wolcott right in there behind them." ATV seem to feel that way. They're putting W.C.Wolcott in there this week on no less than three consecutive nights. Four hours long in all, the show is a fast-moving curtain-raiser to a planned 13-part series.

The setting is Hackney in London's East End where Det.Constable Wolcott, fresh out of uniform and anxious to make waves is assigned to keep the peace at street level in a tough, race-conscious city. "He's not a crusader, just a cop doing his duty," says Harris. "He's in the middle. A loner. He just happens to rub everyone up the wrong way, including his superiors and colleagues on the force."

Along the busy pavements and street markets where the entire eight-week location was filmed, Harris was the focus of all eyes, tall and slim in his white Alan Ladd raincoat with its shoulder epaulettes, noisome tie, and a stare like a blow-torch. The man stands at 6ft. 3in., none of it fat. He's 33. The face has the fine bone structure and polished dark skin of a Belafonte. The voice is soft and persuasive. "Wolcott's right there in the thick of it," he says. "That's his job. Among the white guys on the force he's a sharp, classy dude, neat and meticulous. Maybe too much so. Among the blacks Wolcott's got to make his own way, show them they can trust him. He's got tremendous integrity and nothing can shake him. He stays cool."

William Hall, *TV Times*, 1981

Wolcott. Photo courtesy of Thames Television

Britain's answer to Sidney Poitier

Wolcott, ATVs homemade answer to all those over-wrought Best Sellers from Hollywood, is somewhat less glossy than its precursors in the Tuesday-through-to-Thursday blockbuster slot. It leans further over towards fact and some of its facts are nasty ones: corruption, violence and racism in a North London community and particularly in its police force.

Winston Churchill Wolcott is your traditional straight baddie-hating cop who has just been promoted from the beat to the CID. To most of the black community he is a 'token nigger' who has sold out to the enemy; to many of his colleagues, he's an uppity one who needs to be told his place. The storyline, basic cops v hoodlums and delinquents, is slightly slowed by the necessity to fill in the sociological details for a television audience mostly used to seeing black actors as shallow stereotypes, there just to help the action along.

But the detail is one of *Wolcott*'s strengths. As a Socialist Worker mounts a soapbox to explain to shoppers in Brixton Market that racism fatally divides a working class which should be united and the National Front ripostes with crude slogans of hate, you see the familiar on the screen and realise that there it is unfamiliar. And in the reactions of the blacks there's no romantic response. The argument, you are made to feel, is like that of two dogs squabbling over a bone long since snatched by a third: irrelevant and too late.

The script of *Wolcott* is by two American writers, Barry Wasserman and Patrick Carroll, who settled in Britain some years ago and both of whom live in multi-racial areas of London. They wrote it as a screenplay but were unable to find anyone willing to make the film. Eventually the script landed on the desk of Jacky Stoller, a producer with Black Lion Films, a subsidiary of ATVs parent company, ACC.

"I liked it because it is modern; it is about the eighties. The social comment is not window-dressing; it is the background on which the story hinges and which motivates the characters. It is an integral part of a good story and immensely interesting. I learned a lot just from reading the script and much more from working with the black actors and on the Hackney locations," she says.

Like most intelligent middle-class men and women, Jacky was aware of racism, aware that it was an evil and ready to condemn it. But it was an abstract; through making *Wolcott* she has seen its concrete unreason and malice. "I want the people who watch *Wolcott* to see that too," she says. "I think that sometimes drama can educate more effectively than documentary. Certainly it has the opportunity to educate more people because its audience is wider. But it also has the facility to make people identify with characters from an alien and previously misunderstood group and that can lead to sympathy for the group."

"It can even," she adds with a smile, "lead to social and economic change. Friends in Oxford told me recently that their cleaning woman had come to them and announced that, since the charlady in *Coronation Street* was being paid £1.50 an hour, didn't they agree that 75p an hour was rather stingy and ought to be improved upon."

There has been no attempt in *Wolcott* to twist the truth or make propaganda by making more blacks than should be goodies or more whites baddies – though when Winston Wolcott arrives at his new station, his reception is so hostile, you discover you are anxiously willing just *one* of the whites to be a nice guy. Three give our hero a smile and guilt feelings are relieved.

The Metropolitan force, which does boast 83 people of ethnic minorities on its strength, is said to be none too happy about *Wolcott*, but there is nothing in it that careful reading of the newspapers and an evening listening to a South London social worker will not have made you already aware of. "Of course," says Jacky, "you have to heighten some of the dramatic content to make it acceptable on a viewing level. All art, on whatever level, has to select and emphasise."

Brenda Polan, *The Guardian*, 13 January 1981

Not since *Roots* by Alex Hayley have we been treated to the kind of black television blitz that ATV's *Wolcott* gave us from 13 January through to 16 January 1981. And, in its January issue, *West Indian World* boasted that we had at last in Britain, our first real black TV star in George Harris. George was the star of *Wolcott*, a four-part cops and robbers drama which swamped for three nights solid with a double dose (2 hours) on the final night. *Wolcott* aimed to provide the nation with an acute, closely observed, but entertaining picture of the inner-city, black

Wolcott. Photo
courtesy of
Thames
Television

Traditional, straight, baddie–hating cop promoted to the CID

community – the 'natives' mainly at play, and hardly ever at what you'd call work.

WHOSE IMAGE?

So blacks appear to have here, a chance of jobs for black actors, and at last, a chance to see our community portrayed in a multi-faceted kind of way. One supposes that all blacks should be happy about this. And indeed many of us will have been so happy to see ourselves reflected in the great TV eye, which normally looks straight through us like we weren't here, that our first response might have been one of pleasure. And in *Wolcott*, we weren't even painted all black, as so often happens – some of the black characters were painted almost white. (In fact all of them were – as usual). And if the series takes off, soon every nigger could be a star – but at what cost? Stars made in whose image?

For years we've complained that we are grossly under-represented in TV drama, documentary and popular entertainment. And for years our actors have complained that they should be offered full character parts, rather than female servants, studs, and crowd fillers. But if *Wolcott* is a sign of the band-wagons being offered for exposure and stardom – we must refuse, and so must our actors.

Wolcott was written and produced to a formula, and although it looked as though it was shot on location in London's black community, it was really not about nor in the interests of any part of the black communities in Britain. Black viewers will have recognised the faces, but not the lines – black youth don't sit in parks chanting "pig, pig, pig, pig. . ." when police, black or white walk past. Black viewers will have recognised the ghetto predicaments, but not the events portrayed – we don't have an everyday 'junkie' problem amongst black youth in Britain; nor do we have a black mafia organising youth to mug and stab little old white ladies, for the pittance in their handbags.

CONDEMNED

Wolcott is a fictional black cop. But *Wolcott* could also be the best walking advertisement yet devised to attract black people into the police force. It is to be remembered that ever since ex-police chief and star of the Spaghetti House siege, Robert Mark, started a campaign to recruit black police in 1972 – spending as much as £25,000 on it in 1975 – the Force has failed to attract many more than a couple of hundred black police. With *Wolcott* we see everything being thrown in to present a recruitment pitch. The bent copper is portrayed. Racist coppers are shown, verbally abusing black, even the black in uniform. And *Wolcott* is shown as a man sensitive to all these abuses and corruptions, and militantly defensive of his blackness – but still with a mind for being a cop. And the basis on which this trick is turned, is the misrepresentation and criminalisation of the entire black community. One supposes that the argument of the nice, white, liberal

TV writers and producers, who made *Wolcott*, must be, that since black youth are all criminal, then in order to get them policed by other than vindictive, brutal, white racist cops, black people who care about law and order, and morality, should consider joining the police. Who are they kidding? The police in Britain have shown themselves to be *not* accountable to the black community. That is why we already protest against the intention to grant extended police powers, as recommended recently by the Royal Commission on Criminal Procedure. Black people cannot, in all consciousness, join such a police force. (See, 'Police Against Black People', I.R.R. 1979)

STEREOTYPES

The producer, Jacky Stoller, is reported to have said, "I think that sometimes drama can educate more effectively than documentary." Too true – and hence the more serious concern of the present argument. Ms Stoller believes that she "learned a lot just from reading the script and much more from working with the black actors and on the Hackney locations" (*Guardian* January 1981). One doesn't know how much say the black actors had, but the script was written by two Americans settled in Britain. It showed, Ms Stoller admits, further, that her art, indeed "All art, on whatever level, has to select and emphasise." So what does this art teach us? She presented us with a series of stagey, black stereotypes – our youth were made out to be wayward, muggers and murderous with parents absent or unable to cope with them, in a community full of black mafia type gangsters. In order to establish these, we had the US 'junkie' problem presented as a UK black youth problem – kids with needles, stretched out in youth club toilets, and dying in their beds. We had black women represented as either ineffectual or strong but confused or as prostitutes. We had militant, political blacks treated dismissively, and shown as irrelevant to the black youth predicament.

This Americanisation of the black experience in Britain, misrepresented us, criminalised us, and treated us irresponsibly and with disrespect. Even if we go to church, our community still sins all the same. Of course, there were also white baddies portrayed as stereotypes – but we don't have to be as concerned about these misrepresentations, (apart from the celebration of gratuitous violence through them) because the majority of white viewers won't be fooled by them as easily. They have a wealth of certain knowledge that all whites are not like that. About blacks, they know nothing but what they are told and what the camera shows them, interpreted through their ignorant fears and their racism.

Wolcott. Photo courtesy of Thames Television

Misrepresents and criminalises the black community

'FRAME-UP'

The little details of language, and style, and location, in *Wolcott* were designed to convey realism, but the overall picture they were made to fit into was false. It was, effectively, a frame-up. But what are we being framed-up for? What is the consequence of the entire nation, night after night, being presented with this picture of a degenerate black community. A community which clearly can't be sorted out by one or even a few black cops, no matter how worthy, well-meaning and talented. *Wolcott* is shown to be, all the time, fighting a heroic but finally a losing battle with his people. These criminal and degenerate ghettos can't be cleaned up by even a division of *Wolcotts*. This deeply immoral and confused community is too far gone for even the missionary police, black or white. It's a situation that calls for firm, creative, liberty-taking policing. The picture painted of the fictional black community promotes the idea that between the law-abiding citizen and these monsters in the ghetto, stand the police.

Meanwhile in real life the police look like winning the powers to place communities so defined under siege. Blacks are threatened with the real possibility of being prisoners in the streets. From time to time the SPG has done dry runs along these lines. And the nation, indeed the world, having been sold pictures like those painted in *Wolcott*, will have been prepared for the necessity to clamp down even further on blacks – perhaps even with regular police occupations of our communities from time to time. Four hours of dramatic misrepresentation piled into three nights of TV – is bad news for blacks. Very effective because the audience is not used to seeing blacks on TV.

Part of the way out of this situation could involve employing more black writers and producers for TV – but that won't be enough in itself. The new writers and producers black or white must be responsible and respectful of the black community, and conscious of anti-racist imperatives. *Wolcott* happens to have been done by a white production team, but it could have been done by blacks too. Take for example what, at first sight appears to be an unrelated academic exercise carried out about two years ago. In 1978 a black sociologist (Afro-Caribbean) came to Britain, researched the Bristol black community, and wrote an apparently liberal and sympathetic Ph.D. on the St. Paul's community. The book was called *Endless Pressure*. His conclusions could have been the 'scientific' background to the *Wolcott* fiction. He talked about a community of 'saints' and hustlers and teenyboppers, and 'inbetweeners' under such 'endless pressure' that it was unfortunately but undoubtedly a degenerate community. It was this same community that was obliged to rise in April 1980, to defend itself against a massive police occupation which the authorities tried to justify in terms of a 'criminal' black community. Say no more.

Imruh Caesar, Henry Martin, Colin Prescod, Menelik Shabazz, *Grass Roots*, March 1981

THE CHINESE DETECTIVE

THE CHINESE CONNECTION

John Andrew Ho, the Chinese detective, is 25, a Detective Sergeant in Limehouse, the fog-draped haunt of sinister Chinese villains in Victorian novels. Yip wandered about there before work began on the series. "The dock area reminded me of Liverpool. The people look stunned. It has a dying smell." In fact, despite talk of the need for minority representation, height restrictions tend to keep the Chinese out of the police. "But there must be at least one Chinese policeman in London," says David Yip. "I saw him on the news when they showed the Chinese New Year celebrations in Gerrard Street. John Ho is trying to find himself outside the strict rules of the Chinese community he was born to. I think he suddenly said one day: 'I'm a Londoner, too'." Ho has another reason for joining the police, a mission connected with his father's past which is revealed in the first episode of the series. He is totally determined, but also quiet and gentle: far from the classic macho detective of television. His thoughts, background and reactions are quite different from those of his police colleagues – he is, inevitably, an outsider. David Yip feels very strongly about British casting traditions. He is on the Afro-Asian Committee of the actors' union, Equity, which has been fighting for integrated casting on merit for years. "People will say it's not realistic to have a black man playing a white. Then you get white actors blacking up – Othello, for example. In *On the Buses* the characters were all white – public transport would come to a halt without blacks." A point the committee has made about the subsidised theatres is that non-whites are paying their taxes too, to support them: "What are they doing to reflect society?" Kids who are black or any other colour need fictional images to relate to. And actors, Yip feels, are themselves powerful images in our society. But progress has been made. This new series could not have been made, Yip says even three years ago. He was thrilled when he read the pilot script. "I've sat here thinking, 'I'm not getting the parts, should I write something? What would I write?' I just shook at the way Ian Kennedy Martin – a white guy – had caught everything I have dreamed about." David Yip has thought a lot about what being Chinese means. "I have come to the conclusion, that the Chinese are everyone's favourite foreigner."

Radio Times, 25 April 1981

The Chinese Detective. Photo courtesy of BBC

Delightful thumbing of noses at all the cop–show conventions

Should anyone award a prize for most Audacious Programme 1982, when the gong-giving season next comes around, the prime candidate is now declared. Not the nude and naughty *OTT*. Not some *Panorama* reporter's appalling cheek in allowing a Tory heretic to air his un-Thatcherite view. *The Chinese Detective* (BBC1) is leader of the field.

Consider the case. This unassuming set of yarns revolves about one of the shorter members of the Met, a Detective Sergeant, name of Ho, whose patch seems to stretch roughly from Limehouse, where S.Holmes met the Yellow Peril in opium dens of yore, to the south edge of Soho, stamping ground, the popular sheets do say, of the Triads.

Not that his sleuthing activities have any racial restriction – unlike some of his clients' minds, of course. Nursed through one series in BBC1's Sunday night potting shed, *The Chinese Detective* proved to be a rather cunningly crafted piece of work, created by Ian Kennedy Martin somewhere between the BBC's new popular romantic vein – *Shoestring*, *Bergerac* – and Kennedy Martin's old and grittier *Z Cars* beat.

But now what do we find? The humble Ho is daring to drive his slovenly Morris in a Friday night slot where once Starsky and Hutch, and even Kojak for a while, reigned slickly supreme. Friday night is action night, from *It's A Knockout* to the late, late – well, half past eleven sometimes – movie. And what does *The Chinese Detective* offer to set our juices flowing? Oh, it was a car chase all right. It began with gunfire in a deserted warehouse even Regan of *The Sweeney* wouldn't have braved alone; continued as the baddies car zoomed from top floor concealment, screeched down the ramps, burst on to the streets with our hero now in hot pursuit and ended, with all the right grinds and bumps, as the escaper met the inevitable 12-wheeler proceeding in the transverse direction.

What gave this chase a flavour Kojak never got from his lollipop, however, was that the baddie was a gent of 73 whose intended victim was not our Ho but another septuagenarian with whom he'd had a tiff, and that the whole tyre-screeching episode was played out not in supersprung Chevvies but the sort of nifty little three-wheelers we once called bubble cars.

Moreover, within seconds the grouchy victim was cradling the hitman's head in his arms, and leaving Ho without any witness to the escapade. It was a delightfully cocky thumbing of noses at all the cop-show conventions yet, played for all it's worth, it was exciting even while provoking giggles.

The tale of friends who fell out – and the old couple were most delicately played by Nat Jackley and Maurice Denham – was just one strand in the episode, with John, Ho's own father and the trial of the corrupt cop who framed him (where the last series ended) providing another with opportunities for widening the area of comment and hardening the programme's edge.

The confidence of Ian Kennedy Martin's script and Ian Toynton's direction allowed the characterisation here to develop from the barest hints, and there is always a strong sense of place and of today's life – racism and all. This script seems tougher than I remembered the earlier ones in that respect and David Yip's cool and engaging performance gives Ho a range of responses notably smiling almost lovingly as though to his own Dad, his deflating reply to an outburst from Maurice Denham: "Because you're a boring old fascist."

Peter Fiddick, *The Guardian*, 11 September 1982

WIDOWS

MORE DEADLY THAN THE MALE

A hold-up van explodes and kills three professional criminals. Their widows inherit plans for a £1 million robbery. Could they pull the job themselves? Here, the author of this major new ITV drama series gives personal histories of the three members of the gang and a fourth recruit.
by Lynda La Plante

DOLLY RAWLINS
Aged 46

Educated Morpeth Street
Secondary Modern and Coburn
Grammar School, both East
End of London

Dolly's wedding was in a registry office, a quiet, simple ceremony. She would have married Harry Rawlins on the top of a double-decker bus if he'd asked. Dolly and Harry grew up together. She had always admired him, his strong personality and his handsome looks. He had played the field but he always went back to Dolly. She never looked at anyone else. Harry liked that. He also liked her taste, her basic intelligence – she was, after all, a grammar school girl. Dolly gave up her job in a lawyer's firm, where she was the receptionist and telephonist, and made her home a mirror of herself: tasteful, clean, neat. Dolly had to guide Harry's taste to begin with, but he learned fast. As he grew more powerful Dolly was content to remain in the background.

Their house was like a palace. Harry took care to protect it, as he protected Dolly, as if she was part of his growing status, and she never let him down. Harry would still ask Dolly's opinion on business 'friends' even on small 'bits of business' and she was always right. She seemed to have an instinctive ability to know who to trust. Above all, Harry knew he could trust her even with his life. Harry *was* Dolly's life; she asked for nothing more, she needed nothing more and her love never faltered. The girls on the till at the local supermarket would give the eye to the manager when she came in, and he would be ready and waiting to help her unload the contents of her trolley into a box – at once. A few years back, Dolly had stood ready to pay, a load of shopping waiting to be carried out, and she had let rip. . . "What? Pay for a plastic bag when I'm spending 45 quid? Pay for a bag with your adverts all over it? Do me a favour – get me the manager, and tell 'im to bring a box!" Dolly had refused to pay out a penny until her shopping was neatly packed into boxes. She then handed over the cash and left. The manager walked docilely after her, placed the boxes carefully in her car and got a fiver for his trouble. From then on Mrs Rawlins never had to ask. . .

SHIRLEY MILLER
AGED 23

Educated Paddington Green
Primary School and St George's
Comprehensive, Maida Vale, London

Shirley married Terry Miller when she was 16. The wedding was very flash. She wore a white lace dress with a twenty foot train. Her brother Greg got so drunk he went missing for three days. There was a champagne reception for more than a hundred guests. Even the lace handkerchief her mother Audrey sobbed into had been paid for by Terry. Shirley forgot about her dream of entering the *Miss World* competition – she was too houseproud and busy setting up home. Terry did his best to provide anything she wanted. He watched his child-bride blossom into a woman, into a wife any man could be jealous about. Shirley never asked about business. She had once, had seen him close up like a clam and decided it was better to leave the subject alone. Audrey came round only when invited and would look with hungry eyes at her daughter's neat, immaculate house. Audrey had never had more than a council flat, never had money to spare for household gadgets. Audrey knew exactly what Terry did for a living. He was a villain, one of the heavy mob. One day she brought the subject up and was almost frightened by her daughter's reaction. Shirley whipped round on Audrey and told her that if she ever mentioned it again she would never set foot in her house, never see her again. "He's everything I ever wanted. I love him. I want his kids. Nothing you say, or anyone else says makes any difference – I love him" . . . Audrey never mentioned it again.

LINDA PERELLI
Aged 26

Educated Thomas Coram
Foundation, London, and Doctor
Barnardo's, The Village,
Barkingside, Essex.

Linda was brought up by three sets of foster parents, her mother having left her in Doctor Barnardo's when she was three. Various odd jobs took her to the West End of London where she met Italian Joe Perelli in a night club. She lived with him for three-and-a-half years before she got him to marry her. It hadn't been easy, but no matter how he had treated her she refused to budge. Once she lay down across the front door, shouted at him to walk all over her, but she wasn't going to leave him. He stepped over her and went out until morning. When Joe was away from her he used to wonder how he ever got himself involved in the first place. Then he would laugh; she always made him laugh. Linda was hopeless in the kitchen. Once she had tried to make spaghetti. She had read in a woman's magazine that if you throw a piece of spaghetti on the ceiling and it sticks, the pasta is ready to serve. Her sleeve caught on the pan handle and Joe found Linda covered in spaghetti, the walls and ceiling plastered with it.

One night he threw her out, battered suitcase and all. After two hours he went in search of her and found her drunk, propped up in a bar, singing *Ave Maria*. He knew then that he loved her – but marry her? His family never forgave him. Joe spent his money like water. If Linda was around when he had it then she would get a share, if she wasn't it would go on horses, dogs, even the odd whore, but if she ever questioned his life style, he would blow like a time-bomb. He was a typical Italian; Linda was his property. She was his wife. She must be above reproach. And she was. She kept her nose clean, behaved herself. She was proud of Joe and she loved to see people's faces when she mentioned his name. "Oh, you know Joe do you? Well, I'm his missus. I'm Joe Perelli's old lady."

BELLA O'REILLY
Aged 28

Educated St Boniface School and
Convent of the Holy Family,
Balham, London

Bella, widowed when her husband died of a drug overdose, is recruited into the team by Linda. Black, tall and 'well-stacked', she is a stripper and a prostitute. She never knew her father, a travelling salesman. Her mother was a dancer who danced spasmodically through her daughter's life with a trail of 'uncles', and Bella was brought up by her grandparents in Balham. Bella saw her future husband Don winning a local disco dance competition. Somehow or other she never really made it home again. There was never a dull moment when Don was around. Bella began dancing, entering competitions with him as her partner. They dreamed of becoming professionals, but the dream remained always around the corner, and the corner got further and further away as Don started dealing in drugs. Bella began dancing alone in the clubs. At first she wouldn't strip, but the money was good so she thought, 'What the hell. . .'. Don was jailed for three years. When he got out he was different. He was jealous of her, but at the same time encouraged her to make even more money – he was now on heroin. "Just the odd punter," he would say. Once, when he was high, he brought home a marriage certificate and they married at Lambeth Registry Office. Don spent the next few years in and out of prison. Bella was always waiting for him, but, it was like having a sick child on her hands. Then the drugs caught up with him. . .

TV Times, 12–18 March 1983

Racial difference is marked in a range of ways

BELLA

She claimed sexual and racial prejudice with the production crew of the series, but she was more emotional and upset about that than depressed. (Mr Anthony Earlham, stepfather of Eva Mottley, quoted by *The Times* in its report on the post-mortem of Ms Mottley, 21 March 1985)

Although all publicity for *Widows* showed four women, three white, one black, in the first episode we are introduced only to the three white women, widows of the men who died in the underpass raid. Of course, we later learn that Dolly Rawlins, one of these women, was not in fact widowed in the raid, the third widow was in fact Jimmy Nunn's wife, Trudie. The fourth widow of the credits, Bella O'Reilly, is recruited by her friend, Linda Perelli, in the second episode. The original three have discovered that they will need a fourth, and Bella's suitability occurs to Linda when her co-worker, Charlie, comments of Bella that "she looks too much like a fella", to be attractive. It has earlier been established that Bella too is now a widow ("My old man did the final load three months ago") and is working as a prostitute and in strip clubs. It is for this work that Dolly abuses her ('tart', 'slag') when first introduced, but there is no racial abuse for Bella in the first series as there is for the 'rhymed' Afro-Caribbean male character Harvey in the second. He cannot comment that a uniform is a bit small without being called 'ape man', and is shown to be recruited to Harry's gang only as a last resort. In the first series, it is only when Bella is taken for a man that she is referred to as black, by a security guard and the police, trying to identify "the black bloke" after the Widows' raid.

There is no verbal discourse on race in the first series, although racial difference is marked in a range of ways (see below). The second series introduces two new Afro-Caribbean characters, Harvey Rintle, and a girl-friend of Bella's, Carla, as well as a stereotypical Jewish antique-dealer 'fence' (pawnbroker figure), Sonny Chizzel. It also returns to a more conventional 'realist racism'. Harvey becomes the site for the display of the normal and casual racism (realism) of the Rawlins world, threatened because he has a relationship with a white woman and subjected to *Black and White Minstrel Show* jokes when he joins the gang. Carla is mistaken for Bella, and brutally beaten up in the second episode of the second series. When Bella tells the others of this, she loses her temper with Linda for failing to grasp the racist element in the attack: "Of course he did (think it was Bella) – I'm black, she's black, we all look alike in the dark, stupid bitch!" This comment works very curiously with the most noticeable feature of the Bella character, which is that she is played by two different actresses: Eva Mottley and then in the second series, Debby Bishop. This substitution, itself uncommon in British television drama, stands in relation to the national, unsympathetic and uninformative coverage of Eva Mottley's death in February 1985, shortly before *Widows* 1 was repeated, and several months after she left the set at the beginning of shooting *Widows* 2.

The crime series offers particular problems for the representation of race if the production company wishes to move away from the stereotypical presentation of black villains. The problem lies in the way in which the effect of realism is created in a genre. If we take what we might call the internal realism of the genre – its inter-textuality, its construction of the 'reality effect' through particular codes and conventions – the way in which realism as an effect has more to do with the reality constructed in other crime series than with reality as such (out there), we can only conclude that sympathetic characters are white. There are exceptions, like *The Chinese Detective*, but the very title of the series indicates the exceptional juxtaposition of 'Chinese' and 'Detective'. *Wolcott*, with an Afro-Caribbean policeman in the title role, was not extended after the pilot. Sympathetic black characters aren't in this genre at all, except in the USA – they are (or were) over in *Ebony*, *Eastern Eye* and *Black on Black*, or, since *Widows* was first transmitted, in Albert Square. The realist codes and conventions of the genre are homologous with those of television as an institution, in which 'ethnicity' applies only to the non-white.

I am thus suggesting that there is little generic support for Bella as a sympathetic, realist character, which increased the demands made, in the first series, on Eva Mottley as an actress. The strength of her acting was arguably undercut, during the first transmission of *Widows* 1 by the repeated blurring of character and actress in press features. By implication it wasn't acting, it was just natural, as Eva Mottley had served a prison sentence for a drug offence and had started acting while in prison. Bella, in the first series, is characterised as particularly tough. Shirley and Linda are both, in different ways, *girls*. They are quite frequently shown as weak, hysterical, frightened and vulnerable. Dolly, a *woman*, does not reveal the same weaknesses but does have vulnerability in relation to Harry. Dolly is shown to be stern and brusque (one reviewer commented on wishing to cross the road

Widows. Photo
courtesy of
Thames
Television

Debbie Bishop's Bella – very different from Eva Mottley's

to get out of her way), and even slaps the hysterical Linda at a meeting during the second episode. Later in the same episode, in a rhyming gesture, Bella too slaps Linda (who is at that point drunk). It is this gesture which is shown to cause Dolly to reconsider her original rejection of Bella. Bella, in the first series, is never shown to be out of control. The repeated guarantees of 'femininity through vulnerability' which are used in relation to the other widows are not employed in relation to Bella. It is perhaps this uncompromising representation of a strong, cool, tough woman which led to many critics referring to her as 'threatening' and 'androgynous'. It is this latter appellation that is the more revealing, hinting at the proposition that a woman without vulnerability might not be one.

Bella's difference – apart from her later narrative arrival – is most noticeably marked in the opening pre-credit sequence, which partly reflects her different route in. Each week, viewers are brought up-to-date by a male voice over a series of images, some from previous episodes. After Bella's appearance, for episodes three and four the audience is introduced to the widows with an image which offers the simulacrum of a page from a family photographic album. In individual snaps, Linda, Shirley and Dolly appear, not 'now' (alone, or with each other), but with their husbands, happy and relaxed in their socially legitimate past. Bella, on the other hand, appears alone. There are, to an extent, narrative reasons for this – Bella's husband, unlike the others, has no plot significance. To have given Bella the same socially legitimate past, coupleness, could well have been confusing to viewers. But the effect is to mark her difference, to offer her without the visual guarantee of a heterosexual past.

Although all the women were married to criminals, and Linda's job in the amusement arcade is fairly rough, Bella is clearly perceived as less respectable than the others. There seems to be a division between good clean family crime and drugs and sex, with Bella on the dirty side, and this despite the fact that Audrey's first explanation of her daughter Shirley's sudden wealth is that she is 'doing tricks'. Linda asks Bella about her drug use on greeting her, and while Shirley enters for the rather affectionately ridiculed Miss Paddington competition, Bella wears a dog collar, black leather and brandishes a whip to earn money from that favourite post-colonial strip-show theme, black woman as dominatrice.

Debby Bishop, who had worked with Eva Mottley in *Scrubbers* and apparently had Mottley's full support, played a very different Bella. Mottley's Bella had real hauteur and style – she was completely believable at the end of the first series when asked about their celebratory meal: "Book a table? Did I book a table – we are taking over the joint!" In the first episode of the second series, Bella is shown to have become engaged to an evidently rich Brazilian aristocrat who knows nothing of her past. He treats her like a princess, and looks very much like a Mills and Boon hero. Bella – and it is slightly difficult to imagine Mottley in this role, given the strength of the Bella she played – is quite correctly very anxious that her past might catch up with her and ruin her happy ending. This it does, and for the rest of the series Bella is portrayed as one who has loved and lost. In episode four she confides to Dolly, "I reckon I lost my chance." Bishop's Bella, although still tough and at points rather unpleasantly bossy, is vulnerable in ways which make her seem much more like Linda and Shirley. This is partly a quality of performance, but is also a result of the very different narrative structure and positions of power in the second series, in which the women really are more vulnerable.

Charlotte Brunsdon 'Men's Genres for Women' in *Boxed in: Women and Television*, eds. Helen Baehr and Gillian Dyer (Pandora 1987)

BLACK SILK

Ten years ago race on TV was literally a joke – shades of Victorian empire still hung over such insulting parodies as *It Ain't Half Hot Mum* and *Mind Your Language*. Often these were the only visible representations of ethnic minorities on TV – along, that is, with the 'black-as-problem' documentary.

Then blacks and anti-racists got their acts together, and plugged away for a decade through a hundred campaigns, conferences and caucuses. Groups like the Black Media Workers' Association, the Campaign Against Racism in the Media and the black caucus in Equity continually worried away at the BBC and ITV companies in an attempt to get them to drop the colonial mentality. In a sense, a series like *Black Silk* is a progeny of all that anti-racist labour – but for those efforts, it would probably never have been born. Yet the gestation period was too long. While the series is a huge step forward for the BBC, it's come in a way too late. The show, as they say, has moved on.

It's not disparaging to say that one of *Black Silk's* most fascinating features is its opening title sequence. There in twenty brief shots, in forty-five slickly edited seconds, are encapsulated both the dilemma of the central character, black barrister Larry Scott (Rudolph Walker), and the political uncertainty of the series itself. Shot in fetishistic close-up, we see the hands of an affluent, black male (leather gloves, tie, expensive coat, Walkman headphones – yes, even this black man got rhythm) divest himself of his 'everyday' garb, and layer himself self-consciously with the distinctive accoutrements of the British Law (waistcoat, winged shirt, black gown, leather briefcase and, finally, the wig). Only in

*Rudolph
Walker*

the final shot does the camera pull out to a full shot of Larry's face,
gazing classically into the middle distance, like the fifth just man.
Meanwhile, on the soundtrack a lazy, vaguely funky theme tune
(why not reggae or even Elgar? – an ironic case could be made
for either) drives along the transformation.

Here then is the graphic framework – the series' brief, if you
like. This is the story of a privileged, black male and his attempt
literally to take on the institutions of the law, to play the role, to
dress up, to mimic, to integrate. And yet, and yet he can't quite
hack it – the authority is there, the personal power and integrity is
self-evident, but this blackness jars, contrasts too strongly with
the white, starched primness of the shirt. The curly white wig sits
uncomfortably on his black, curly head. He patently doesn't quite
fit.

But the title sequence doesn't tell the whole story. This is not
1975, when white people could get away with defining black

people's lives, when whole cultures could be reduced to the comforting formulae of the sitcom or the soap opera. This series was devised by black playwrite Mustapha Matura and a black lawyer Rudy Narayan (no doubt digging deep into his own casebook). In addition, half the eight episodes were written by black or Asian writers, so there is a sharpness and edge to the narrative, a conviction to many of the issues addressed. Hence, too, the series' explicit condemnation of the racist operation of the law-and-order machine towards ethnic minorities – the savage finality of the Immigration Acts, the arbitrariness of the Prevention of Terrorism legislation and the legal incomprehension of black self-defence efforts.

The characterisation, particularly of the blacks, is also strong for TV drama – for example, Walker himself, Suzette Llewellyn as his daughter, Jasmine, and Feroza Syal as the young Indian wife in Episode 4 (which she also co-wrote). Curiously, it's some of the white characters, particularly in and around the legal profession, who look least at ease, as if they can't quite adjust to their unaccustomed marginality. And, refreshingly, Scott himself is no cool, perfect super-hero – as compensation for his isolated position, he is overweeningly arrogant about his own abilities, (understandably) irritable and bad-tempered, insufferably patriarchal towards his family and contemporaries. Young(ish), gifted and black, but with plenty of warts.

Despite all this, there is a major weakness. And that's the implicit and not dated US-style integrationist logic which informs the series. It's no accident that the opening sequence has precisely a US mini-series feel. You know the kind of thing. . . . you've seen the dutiful black nurse, now here's the upstanding black lawyer, and who knows, in time we may even have a black Prime Minister. But it's a logic, based on notions of personal self-achievement, which never had much credence in Britain – and which is irrelevant to 99% of blacks in this country in 1985, when black communal self-identity is the order of the day.

Carl Gardner, *The Listener*, 31 October 1985

KING OF THE GHETTO

Producer Stephen Gilbert was particularly drawn to *King Of The Ghetto* by the script – written by Farrukh Dhondy, now Channel Four's Commissioning Editor for Multi-cultural Programmes but also responsible for writing popular series like *Tandoori Nights* and *No Problem*. "I think this is a quantum leap for him," says Gilbert. "I compare it to the leap Alan Bleasdale took with *Boys from the Blackstuff*. As well as being a compelling story, it deals directly with important and current material about British society. It's not backward-looking like so much TV drama over the last 15 years."

Zia Mohyeddin endorses Gilbert's view, and sees the series as breaking new ground. 'The apology angle is more or less over. Previous drama about immigrants had a note of apology about it always trying to explain who they were. I think Dhondy has gone beyond that. He's certainly treading on a lot of delicate corns. But these are real characters, not symbols.

"It doesn't feel like ethnic drama" adds director Battersby. There is a range of characters without any question of positive or negative images. For Battersby *King of the Ghetto* is a return to the BBC after a 12 year gap, five of which he devoted to the Workers Revolutionary Party. But he insists 'I work on drama as drama. Politics and drama are linked, but one tries to be faithful to the piece and get as involved as possible, even if it doesn't necessarily reflect one's own political views. As far as I'm concerned *King of the Ghetto* is just a rattling good story."

Not least of Battersby's challenges was casting the Bengali parts. "There's an enormous wealth of talent if you once break through all the different things restricting it," he says. It was also an education for him. In the course of casting he became aware of the easily ignored complexities of the East End Bengali community, let alone the Asian community as a whole (if there is such a thing). "It's the different kinds of layers that are so interesting. And we're trying to reflect that. The young are totally integrated, the older ones are the businessmen, and the oldest ones still speak their own dialects and are very traditional."

The younger Bengalis have a strong desire to get out of their ghetto. Some, like Timur's sharply dressed heavies, Riaz and Raja, have gone 'the American Express route' as Battersby calls it – where the acquisition of goodies is the spur. Public-school educated Aftab Sachak, who plays Riaz, spent a month researching his role: "I talked to the local kids and my character is exactly where they want to be. They want to get out of here, so they want to make money."

For Ajay Kumar, who plays Raja ('a wide-boy on the make'), life in the East End – in the local pool clubs and restaurants – was also a revelation. "You have to be tough here. It's all based on street life." Finding an ethnically suitable cast provided Stephen Gilbert with some unexpected headaches caused by the Race Relations Act. "By law we couldn't advertise for Bengali extras. So we had to advertise for extras who could act Bengalis. As a result, we even had somebody Greek turning up!"

He adds, "While we were making the show, every time we opened the paper, there was something about the kind of material we were shooting. There were attacks on Asian families, the setting up of a Muslim school and rioting in the streets. So we felt very close to real events. And I hope it will feel very much a serial about the current climate."

Radio Times, 26 April–2 May 1986

WHO'S THE KING OF THE GHETTO?

Farrukh Dhondy's drama serial *King of the Ghetto*, which ended recently on BBC2, was a valuable insight into the everday life of a Bangladeshi community in the East End of London. It broke down barriers of misunderstanding between races and blurred the stereotypes by showing whites with a

Not an exercise in public relations for the Bangladeshi community

conscience and blacks without one. So said the white, middle-class critics who write about television.

But the thriller, in which Tim Roth played a white activist leading a Bangladeshi squatters' movement, has stirred up remarkable resentment among both the people it portrays and Britain's black artistic community. Two hundred Brick Lane Bangladeshis demonstrated outside the BBC TV Centre a week ago and, in a letter to several magazines, members of the East End Bengali community called *King of the Ghetto* a third rate drama which "reinforced the racist inclinations of the media".

There was more criticism of Dhondy himself following an interview he gave to the *Screen* pages, before the serial began, in which he bemoaned what he described as a shortage of good black actors in Britain, saying that there were none ready to play 'heavy' roles like Othello.

"It's just not true," says Albie James, a former RSC director who now runs the Temba theatre company. "But we must continue to encourage theatres to bring more black artists through to the top level. If Farrukh does not want to see our national companies reflecting the true nature of our multi-cultural society, he is going the right way about it."

This vehement criticism is embarrassing for Dhondy on two counts. Firstly, he is one of Britain's leading black writers, with a long history of political activism – in the 1960s he joined the Black Panthers and helped organise Bangladeshi squats very like the ones described in *King of the Ghetto*.

More significantly, though, Dhondy is also the Commissioning Editor for Multi-cultural Programmes at Channel 4, charged with the task of nurturing black talent. He denies that the current outcry will make his job at C4 more difficult.

Abdus Shukur, of the Federation of Bangladeshi Youth Organisations, is unimpressed by Dhondy's credentials. "That was a decade ago," says Shukur. "Dhondy was one of those people who dropped into the East End for a brief period to make a political name for himself. He does not come from the community, and he doesn't understand it, which is why *King of the Ghetto* misrepresents us so badly.

"And why did he make us look so thick? In one scene a Bangladeshi woman was being shown how to use a teapot. Bengal is one of the biggest tea-producing regions in the world. Don't you think a woman from there would *know* how to use a bloody teapot?

"All the serial did was to further the idea that it was white activists who came along and got us organised. There *were* whites, but the movement was organised and working before they got there. The just wanted to jump on the bandwagon, and we soon kicked them off."

This makes Farrukh Dhondy very angry. "The man I based the Tim Roth character on lived among the Bangladeshi community for five years, and he sweated blood for them. Some of the people who are complaining probably live in houses he fought to get for them.

"I was writing fiction, but it was based on personal experience. If these people want a public relations job done for them they should put some cash together and send for Saatchi and Saatchi."

As for his remarks about black actors, Dhondy says: "I think my real desire to encourage black artists did not come across in the *Screen* article, which perhaps over-condensed a long and detailed conversation. Albie and I both believe that British theatre must give blacks much greater opportunities, which is one of the things I am trying to do at Channel 4."

James agrees with those who think that white critics were too easy on King of the Ghetto, possibly out of desire to demonstrate their racial understanding. "Black artists don't need patronising praise when we know we're not good enough," he says. "Farrukh obviously believes that too, because at Channel 4 he has turned away several black writers whose work apparently doesn't meet the standard he is looking for.

"There may be another reason, of course. Maybe it is too much of a challenge for one man to be writing and commissioning so much. You see more of Farrukh's work on television than any other black writer's, and that is dangerous. He shouldn't be asked to stop writing, but his objectivity must *not* be affected by his own tastes. Too many others are in danger of being turned away."

Patrick Stoddart, *Sunday Times*, 11 June 1986

NEW STEREOTYPES

Brick Lane on a Sunday morning is a haven for those searching for cheap clothes, cheap furniture and cheap curry. Indian restaurants full with white couples carrying eastern looking carpets to furnish their flats in the Docklands, the Golf GTI's and BMW's line the pavements. By 2pm they have all gone; Brick Lane to them is a nice memory. But for the local Bengali community it has become a wasteland again. The boarded up exteriors conceal the clutter of sweat-shops run by Bengalis and the wall-to-wall corrugated iron conceals the tombs that were once homes. In the mid-seventies the East End hit the headlines with the Brick Lane race riots and the 'paki-bashing' which culminated with the murder of Altaf Ali and Ishak Ali in 1978.

This era was revisited in BBC2's thriller *King of the Ghetto* starring Tim Roth and written by Commissioning Editor for Multi-cultural Programmes for Channel 4, Farrukh Dhondy. Roth played an anarchistic skinhead who took up the cause of the dispossessed Bengalis establishing a squatting and self-help movement. Dhondy an ex-activist, described as a "combination of Svengali, Rasputin and a male Eartha Kitt" by Kathy Myers in *City*

Limits, was born in Poona in 1944 and educated at Pembroke College, Cambridge. In 1967 he joined the Black Panthers – a movement that flashed dangerously through British and American politics, associated with figures such as Malcolm X and Eldridge Cleaver. Dhondy's list of credits are extensive. He has written a number of books (including *East End at Your Feet*). His TV career embraces *Tandoori Nights, No Problem* and *Party Night at the Palace* and he has written plays such as *Vigilantes* for the Asian Cooperative Theatre. In the mid-seventies, a job for *Race Today* took him into the Bengali Community, and it is this experience which provides the subject matter for *King of the Ghetto.*

The play is a scathing denunciation of the exploitation of the political climate for profit-making by Bengali community leaders in the characters of Timur and Riaz. However what Dhondy presents is another stereotype: the corrupt Asian businessman climbing up the ladder of local government politics by using the Asian community. The vote of the Asian community has long been recognised by the Labour party as one to which they can turn even if they fail to help the community in the end. In *Ghetto* this political ladder climbing reflects a mentality that thinks 'lets put an Asian in a safe ward and we'll get those illiterate Bengalis to vote for him with the aid of his heavies'. It was clear from the use of the Muslim schools theme, that the play was set in the eighties but the subjects Dhondy used suited his own experiences of Asians in the seventies. Why is the issue of white leadership still being discussed? The way Asian youth have organised in the past years – evident in the Bradford 12 and Newham 8 trials of the past few years – was completely ignored by Dhondy; the only reference made to the struggles and achievements was in the last scene, where we saw the Bengali youth throwing molotov cocktails at the barricades.

In reality Asian youth in Tower Hamlets have long recognised that the only way to change things in their borough is to be in the places of power. Change, they feel can effectively be achieved through access to existing political structures. Local government is a crucial arena, yet, Dhondy makes a mockery of this throughout the play.

When the East End Bengali community responded to the play, they were understandably critical. "People are annoyed at the consistently superficial portrayal of a community with which the writer has had no links whatsoever in the last ten years", wrote the Federation of Bengali Youth League.

Another area of concern is the way Dhondy and other so-called liberal playwrights portrayed Asian women in their plays – both patronising and at times degrading. The images are nearly always negative in the form of submissive and passive women. Take Shelly King's portrayal of Nasreen – Timur's mistress. She is shown to be an opportunist, willing to jump into bed with anyone as long as she achieves what she wants. She ends up marrying Matthew so that she can stay in this country, having slept with Timur who provided a roof over her head. It may be true that some women resort to such desperate measures, but the point here, especially in the context of the media, is that the only female Asian character in the series is not capable of a sustained relationship. The vagaries of the immigration laws dominate her character. The only steady relationship we see in the play is Matthew and Sadie's. We never see any other Asian women in the play who combat any stereotype this society has of Asian women. The absence of strong Asian women in the play can be blamed on the fact that the play was not about the Bengali community but about Matthew and Sadie. It revolved around Matthew and what he thought and felt.

Who does Dhondy write his play for? Is it for the new breed of middle-class who will say "what a brilliant piece of film. At last we have got rid of the suffering Asian stereotype of Asian women lagging behind their men-folk". Or is it for the racists who will be able to confirm their images of Asians as illegal immigrants, as passive Asians? Such works, including those of Hanif Kureishi (*My Beautiful Laundrette*) create new stereotypes for the Asian community to fight against. Kureishi's women are 'Rita Wolf' type characters; rebellious Asian women who have reached a new extreme where they can flash their breasts at a room full of men. Has Dhondy forgotten the emergence of strong, independent Asian women?

Ghetto, like *My Beautiful Laundrette*, used an ex-skinhead as a main character. Both characters 'flirted' with racism without ever really knowing what they were doing. The fact that we had a skinhead leading the Asian community in the East End was unbelievable, offensive and degrading. Moreover the issue of racism, the violence of the racists, was trivialised thereby ignoring the struggles of the South Asian Community. Such works, despite intentions to the otherwise, reinforce all the stereotypes of our people. More importantly, they create new ones.

Fatima Salaria, *Artrage*, Issue 17, 1987

SOUTH OF THE BORDER

DOWN DEPTFORD WAY

Pearl Parker is black, beautiful and ambitious. Finn Gallagher's a streetwise sneak thief. Together they're an unlikely partnership to follow Cagney and Lacey in pursuit of villainy and injustice.

Even more offbeat is the setting for Parker and Gallagher's mean streets of crime. Not New York, not LA, but Deptford, south-east London.

"Television is always showing us the back streets of Los Angeles, and quite frankly I find the back streets of Deptford far more interesting," says Susan Wilkins, the main writer on *South of the Border*, BBC1's new eight-part serial. "I wanted to say: look – it's quite possible for two girls living on an estate in Deptford, who are just ordinary people, to get into exciting things.

"There's this idea that ordinary people who live in Deptford aren't interesting, unless it's a gritty realism about heroin being shot up, but my 'manor', as the boys would say, is an incredibly vibrant area.

"It's multi-racial and multi-cultural, the stuff of drama," she adds with relish. "An area where things are going on . . . all kinds of scams, people making a living in all sorts of ways."

Both Pearl (played by Buki Armstrong) and Finn (Rosie Rowell) begin the serial looking for a new way of making a living. Pearl has just turned her back on a disastrous love affair. Finn has emerged from prison after two years for theft. Pearl is out to put the world to rights: she has a real sense of justice, though it is not

110

always the same as other people's. Finn is noted for her ability to break into almost anything, especially other people's cars.

With the help of their friend and lawyer Milly (played by Dinah Stabb) a haphazard business venture takes shape. They turn themselves into private detectives with a very individual and not always effective style of operation. And from his soul-and-reggae music shop in Deptford High Street – adorned with graffiti specially commissioned by the BBC – Pearl's charismatic ex-lover Fitz (Brian Bovell) lends a hand occasionally.

Buki Armstrong is thrilled to be playing such a positive, upbeat person as Pearl. "As a kid," she says, "I didn't even think there were black actors and actresses: I can't remember seeing any on the telly. We must push people's thinking forward. We've seen ourselves portrayed as the trouble element for too long."

Centre of operations for the two private detectives is a tower block on the Pepys Estate. From there Wilkins can look over her manor. "You can see the elegant white buildings of Greenwich Naval College, the dome of the Observatory, and the masts of the *Cutty Sark* just by the entrance to the Greenwich foot tunnel. We used that for a roller-skating chase scene," she says.

"Then there's the industrial and dockside landscape of Deptford with its breakers' yards full of dismembered cars, and builders' cranes swinging across the skyline; and Deptford Creek, where one of the characters has an unexpected dip. Further off is the London City Airport, where we've filmed some scenes: it's a lesser known part of London's Docklands."

South of the Border doesn't give south-east London a better break. For the series Susan and producer Caroline Oulton (whose previous BBC1 series was *Thin Air*) seem to have developed their own brand of 'positive discrimination'. "It's been a mixture," says Caroline, "of integrated casting plus the writers and directors specifying actors of particular origins."

For instance, Jamaican-born director Wilfred Emmanuel Jones lives, he says, "in the sort of world where I see black and Asian faces all the time; when we were talking about hiring extras it was natural for me to request a certain number of non-white ones." There is a fair sprinkling of familiar faces, too – Tom Watt (formerly of *EastEnders*) turns up in episode three.

South of the Border looks set to nudge television drama considerably further down the road of racial integration but Susan

Wilkins feels that television has yet to catch up with the realities of our multi-racial society. "One of the things that struck me particularly during the filming, talking to the younger actors, is that among the under-25s there is a racial mix that most people don't suppose is there," she says. "There is a lot of integration in inner-city areas that isn't acknowledged. *South of the Border* recognises that a whole generation has grown up together; to me that's a very hopeful thing."

Pat Rowe, *Radio Times*, 22–28 October 1988

Developed its own brand of positive discrimination

THE SWIGGING DETECTIVES

Philip Marlowe would have approved: the short dark one has the face of a reluctant angel and the soul of a tearaway, the tall one is black, beautiful and as street-wise as a clamping operator.

112

Two private dicks in the making. Female private dicks. Operating from a Council flat in a tower block in South London, almost as shabby as Marlowe's office in downtown Los Angeles.

The regulation swigging from a straight bottle of rye is replaced by cans of lager and no-one carries a gun, but the new drama series from the BBC, *South of the Border*, has a true Chandleresque flavour; pithy wit, a healthy distrust of authority and wealth, and a shrewd acceptance that the law and justice don't always balance out.

The setting is somewhere round Deptford and the two girls, Finn (Rosie Rowell) and Pearl (Buki Armstrong) are out of work: Finn because her unrepentant penchant for helping herself to other people's property would tax the trust of a saint, and Pearl because she has walked out on the lover who was her boss.

It is her suspicions about his two-timing activities that lead her to keep a 72 hour surveillance on him so successfully that she decides detective work is just a matter of diligence and common sense. She negotiates her first job with her driving instructor; if she finds his mistress her fee will be six free lessons.

But she gets more than she bargains for and the girls find themselves right in the middle of a very nasty pornography ring. When Pearl tries to tell the police of its existence she is told that they have neither the time nor the work-force to deal with interfering feminists. Nice touch, that, but there are so many nice touches throughout.

There's a club scene with Pearl's kid brother Rufus (Valentine Nonyela) achieving his ambition to become a DJ, complete with scratch music that is patently authentic and swings magnificently.

Then there's his mum nagging him for wearing his roller-skates indoors and Pearl for having had an affair with a married man. Somehow it makes you feel part of the family. So when trouble happens to Rufus in the form of a car chase with the pornos versus his skates, you really care. Of course it is preposterous, or is it? Dodgy money to make villains of both blacks and whites.

In the second episode the girls team up with Milly (Dinah Stabb), a jauntily cynical legal aid lawyer who accepts that 95 per cent of her clients are guilty as charged but does her best for them just the same. The community expands to include cadaverous cocaine-snorting white ladies who lust after beautiful black boys.

We are spared the full sleaze treatment, but it was at this point that I began to feel sorry for any local estate agents who may be hoping to turn the area (full of tall Victorian abodes just begging for refurbishment) into yuppieland. Particularly as the interweaving theme is about urban foxhunting, a new one on me, but it's a long time since I lived south of the river.

Sandy Fawkes, *London Evening Standard*, 21 October 1988

CREDITS AND TRANSMISSION DATES

GANGSTERS

Written by: Philip Martin
Producer: David Rose
Production Company: BBC
Tx dates: 9.1.75 (Play for Today)
9.9.76–21.10.76 (1st series)
6.1.78–10.2.78 (2nd series)

CAST
Maurice Colbourne (Kline); Elizabeth Cassidy (Anne); Ahmed Khalil; Paul Barber; Alibe Parsons (Sarah Gant); Saeed Jaffrey; Robert Stephens (Sir George Jeavons)

WOLCOTT

Written by: Barry Wasserman & Patrick Carroll
Executive Producer: Barry Hanson
Producer: Jacky Stoller
Production Company: Thames
Tx dates: 13.1.81–15.1.81

CAST
George William Harris (Wolcott); Merdelle Jordine (Cynthia Jerome); Mona Hammond (Mrs Wolcott); Lloyd Anderson (Rev.Jerome); Hugh Quarshie (Dennis St George); Christine Lahti (Melinda Marin) Paul McDowell (Chief-Supt.Cosgrave)

THE CHINESE DETECTIVE

Series created by: Ian Kennedy Martin
Producer: Terence Williams
Story Editor: Joan Clark
Production Company: BBC
Tx dates: 30.4.81–4.6.81 (1st series)
10.9.82–5.11.82 (2nd series)

CAST
David Yip (Det-Sgt John Ho); Peter Joyce (Hospital registrar); Mike Lewin (Sgt Wicks); Shirley Stelfox (Arlene); Jack Le White (Old Harry Rose); Venecia Day (Rose's secretary); P H Moriarty (Rose); Derek Martin (Det Chief Insp Berwick); John Bott (Det Chief Supt Halsey)

WIDOWS

Written by: Lynda La Plante
Executive Producers: Verity Lambert (1st series)
Linda Agran & Johnny Goodman (2nd series)
Producer: Linda Agran (1st series)
Irving Teitelbaum (2nd series)
Production Company: Thames
Tx dates: 16.3.83–20.4.83 (1st series)
3.4.85–8.5.85 (2nd series)

CAST
Ann Mitchell (Dolly Rawlins); Maureen O'Farrell (Linda Perelli); Fiona Hendley (Shirley Miller); Eva Mottley/Debby Bishop (Bella O'Reilly); Kate Williams (Audrey Withey); Maurice O'Connell (Harry Rawlins)

BLACK SILK

Series devised by: Mustapha Matura & Rudy Narayan
Producer: Ruth Boxwell
Production Company: BBC
Tx dates: 7.11.85–26.12.85

CAST
Rudolph Walker (Larry Scott); Kika Markham (Julie Smythe);

KING OF THE GHETTO

Written by: Farrukh Dhondy
Producer: Stephen Gilbert
Director: Roy Battersby
Production Company: BBC
Tx dates: 1.5.86–22.5.86

CAST
Zia Mohyeddin (Timur); Gwyneth Strong (Sadie); Tim Roth (Matthew); Dinesh Shukla (Saliq); Richard Butler (Headmaster); Alec Linstead (Bill); Ajaykumar (Raja); Aftab Sachak (Riaz); Shelley King (Nasreen); Paul Anil (Jamal Ullah); Mohammed Ashiq (Prashar)

SOUTH OF THE BORDER

Written by: Susan Wilkins
Producer: Caroline Oulton
Production Company: BBC
Tx dates: 25.10.88–13.12.88

CAST
Buki Armstrong (Pearl Parker); Rosie Rowell (Finn Gallagher); Brian Bovell (Fitz); Valentine Nonyela (Rufus); Corinne Skinner-Carter (Rose); Kwabena Manso (Denzil); Dinah Stabb (Millie)

116

PART THREE

COMING CLEAN

Soap Operas

INTRODUCTION

Stephen Bourne

For nearly a quarter of a century, until it ended in 1988, the television soap opera *Crossroads* was ridiculed for its bad acting, directing and sets. However throughout its life it was also one of Britain's most popular television programmes. Its success with audiences was proved time and time again by its consistently high ratings and appearances in popularity polls. More importantly, *Crossroads* often attempted to address social issues which other British soaps of the 1960s and 1970s avoided. Needless to say, this series has never been given credit for attempting to break new ground in its representation of 'social problems' (such as Diane Lawton becoming a single parent in 1969) and minority groups.

This may have something to do with the fact that, for many years, British soaps, such as *Coronation Street* and *Crossroads*, were generally ignored and despised by the entertainment profession and academics. Consequently these television programmes, though consistently popular with audiences, were never recognised as 'serious' television drama. It is hardly surprising to find that in the 1970s, when readers were asked to vote for their television favourites in polls conducted by the *Sun* and *TV Times*, the results included the following: in the 1970 *Sun* TV awards readers voted *Coronation Street* the Top Series, and in 1973, 1974 and 1975 they voted *Crossroads* their Top ITV Series three years in a row. Also in 1975 they voted Noele Gordon, the star of *Crossroads*, their Top TV Personality. The poll run by *TV Times* produced similar results: in 1971 readers voted Ena Sharples of *Coronation Street* the Most Compulsive Female

TV Character, and for five consecutive years – between 1971 and 1975 – Noele Gordon was voted their Favourite Female TV Personality. However, it was not until 1980 that BAFTA (British Academy of Film and Television Arts) decided to recognise and honour *Coronation Street* when they presented the series with a 'Special Television Award'.

This was overdue recognition by the 'establishment' of a series which had maintained a high standard of drama on British television for twenty years. Needless to say, BAFTA continued to ignore the many wonderful performances of actors and actresses who appeared in *Coronation Street* until 1987, when they finally nominated Jean Alexander (Hilda Ogden) as Best Actress, unprecedented for a performer in a soap opera. Meanwhile, the British Film Institute published *A Television Monograph* on *Coronation Street* in 1981, which helped to give the series further 'respectability', and made it possible for it to be discussed by lecturers in academic institutions without feeling embarrassed. This was followed in 1982 by Dorothy Hobson's *Crossroads: The Drama of a Soap Opera*.

Coronation Street has been running continuously since 9 December 1960 and has retained its popularity, as well as its conservatism. In its early days, when it was produced in black and white, *Coronation Street* was social realist drama of the highest order, equal to such films as *Saturday Night and Sunday Morning*, though it has never been given credit for this. Needless to say, *Coronation Street* has not been without its shortcomings, and one of the main criticisms of it has been its failure to include black and Asian characters. However, it is not generally known that as far back as 1963, in four episodes from 7–23 January the *Street* included two black characters in one of its storylines. Thomas Baptiste portrayed Johnny Alexander, a bus conductor who was reported by Len Fairclough and given the sack. Len later admitted the accusations were false, but Johnny refused reinstatement on principal. Barbara Assoon also made an appearance in one episode as Johnny's wife.

H.V.Kershaw, *Coronation Street*'s first script editor, and later the serial's producer, and contract writer, later recalled this storyline, and attempted to defend the *Street*'s reluctance to include black and Asian characters, and to avoid what was seen by a succession of producers, as a 'touchy' subject:

120

Thomas Baptiste. Photo courtesy of Granada

Johnny Alexander – sacked bus conductor in Coronation Street

Len Fairclough, accused by a West Indian bus conductor of not paying his fare, reported the incident to his inspector friend Harry Hewitt when he appeared on the scene, with the result that the bus conductor was sacked. Len later admitted that he was in the wrong but the West Indian, when offered his job back, refused to return where he was obviously not trusted. Len and Harry were, quite rightly, the villains of this piece but it is interesting that the *Street* is still criticised for never including black or Asian characters. Blacks and Asians have, in fact, appeared many times although this would never be apparent from our scripts. It has long been a rule that all our coloured characters should be seen to be fully and happily integrated into the community. Which explains why one issue has, apparently, been shirked – namely, that successive producers have been loath to bring a coloured family in the *Street* itself. If this were to be done producers and writers would be forced by the very nature of the show to allow integration to develop at its own pace and to air a mixed bag of opinions on immigration and racialism. I am not alone in believing that such subjects are far too important simply to form one of many themes in a popular drama serial. What is more, in keeping faith with our existing characters, we would again be forced to put unhelpful comment into the mouths of fictional men and women who command a wide following among the serial's millions of viewers, with potentially dangerous effect. It is far easier to inflame the extremists with fictional support for their beliefs than to awaken the consciences of the uncaring with fictional moralities and it would be quite wrong, however strongly well-meaning bodies may urge us to do so, for an entertainment programme to run such risks and accept such responsibility.[1]

Of all the soap operas to have achieved success and popularity in Britain, *Coronation Street* has probably failed more than any other to have represented black and Asian people. H.V.Kershaw's reasons for not doing so are problematic. They expose the racism and ignorance inherent in the series' producers. For years they have resisted suggestions to 'integrate' black and Asian characters into the working-class community portrayed in the programme. There is no evidence to suggest that Asian characters have appeared in the *Street*, and after Thomas Baptiste's appearances in 1963, until the introduction of Lisa Lewis as factory worker Shirley Armitage in 1984, black characters were only seen on very rare occasions, sometimes so briefly that they are now largely forgotten.

Who remembers the two black children fostered by Emily and Ernest Bishop after their marriage in 1972? Or Diana Queesikay's appearances in two episodes as a relief barmaid at the Rovers Return in the mid-1970s? Or the McGregor Brothers, now popularized in a Granada Television sitcom, who made their first television appearance in an episode of *Coronation Street* in 1983 when Eddie Yeats celebrated his engagement party at the Rovers Return? Their creator, John Stevenson, states:

> The two brothers were from Liverpool, and the joke was that when they appeared, one was white and one was black. Annie Walker was outraged because the lads kept saying she reminded them of their mother. They were only cameo roles

but I immediately filed an idea with Granada to develop a comedy series about these two.[2]

Such examples are rare, and to date there have only been two substantial roles played by black performers in the *Street*. In September, 1978, Angela Bruce joined the cast as waitress Janice Stubbs who had an affair with Ray Langton. Says Angela:

Leslie Duxbury wrote ten episodes for me to come in and threaten the marriage of Deirdre and Ray Langton. For the *Street* this was a revolution. In its twenty five year history, black people had never featured. There was one historic moment when a black person threw a dart at the Rovers, but he never said a word. At first the producer Bill Podmore did not want to have me. He said he was worried about racial prejudice, that the viewers might switch off and that the part could easily be done by a white woman. It took months to persuade him, and even when he agreed he wanted me to have bodyguards in case of any adverse reaction. I hoped that I had broken a barrier and this would open the door for other good roles for black actors in the *Street*, but they have since closed up and black people do not really feature.[3]

It was not until 1984 that Lisa Lewis began appearing regularly as Shirley Armitage, one of Mike Baldwin's factory workers. For several years she remained practically silent, with a few lines here and there, and no participation in any stories. For Lewis, a role in the *Street* was a breakthrough in her acting career, but in those early days she was fully aware that her role might never develop. In 1984 she said: "I'm not afraid of being typecast as Shirley because she's such a nice, versatile character. But I think as she's in the factory she's unlikely to develop into a bigger part."[4] However, Shirley Armitage has gradually developed into a central character in the *Street*. In 1988 she became the regular girlfriend of Curly Watts, and soon afterwards they set up home together in the flat above the corner shop. There have also been occasional appearances by Shirley's mother, played by Mona Hammond.

In 1974 Equity's Coloured Artists Committee monitored British television and in the report of their findings entitled *Coloured*

Artists on British Television, published in August, 1974, they criticised the lack of repesentation of black and Asian people in soap operas. Their findings clearly failed to influence the makers of *Coronation Street*. However, three months after the publication of the report, a black family was introduced into *Crossroads*. They were by no means the first black characters to appear in the series. In 1968 Cleo Sylvestre was first seen as Meg Richardson's foster daughter Melanie Harper. Cleo played this role on and off for several years, and became so identified with the character that she would often be recognised and stopped in the street by fans of the series who would ask her for her autograph. Cleo's appearance in *Crossroads* in the late 1960s was a breakthrough, for at that time roles for black actresses in British television were almost non-existent. Her popularity with *Crossroads* fans was such that, for a brief period, she became something of a household name and a celebrity, a rare experience for a black performer in British television at that time.

*Cleo Sylvestre.
Photo courtesy
of ITC*

*Melanie Harper – Meg Richardson's
foster daughter in Crossroads*

In November, 1974, Trevor Butler signed a contract with ATV to appear in *Crossroads* for twenty weeks as Winston James, a juvenile delinquent who runs away from home, and his strict father. The conflict with his father Cameron James, played by Lee Davis, was eventually resolved, thus putting an end to the storyline and the characters. Elizabeth Adare also appeared in the cast as Winston's sister Linda. In August, 1977, *Crossroads* introduced an Asian family, the Chaudris. Meena Chaudri (Karan David) worked at the motel and fell in love with white Dennis Harper (Guy Ward). For an episode transmitted on August 30 1977 the *TV Times* summarised the storyline: "Mr Chaudri explains to his daughter Meena why a future with Dennis Harper is impossible." Renu Setna played Mr.Chaudri, and his wife was played by Jamila Massey. Said television critic Margaret Forward:

> The whole thing reminds me of a story over three years ago in Thames Television's now defunct soap opera *Marked Personal*. It was about an Indian girl who yearned for the same freedom as English girls, but her father held rigid views about how Indian girls should behave, and did not like her taking a job where she would meet English boys. The girl was played by Karan David. The father by – you've guessed it – Renu Setna. If *Crossroads* cannot claim any originality for their plots, they might at least aim for a little originality in their casting.[5]

More than a decade after this observation was made, history is repeating itself yet again in not one, but two British soap operas. At the time of writing (February, 1989) BBC television's *EastEnders* has schoolgirl Shireen (Nisha Kapur) in conflict with her father Mantel (Pavel Douglas) over her relationship with her white boyfriend Ricky, and desire to be 'English', while over on Channel Four in *Brookside*, Nisha (Sunetra Sarker) in in conflict with *her* father Balkrishna (Mohammed Ashiq) over her wish to have the same kind of freedom enjoyed by her English friends. It is interesting to note that Nisha's mother in *Brookside* is played by – you've guessed it – Jamila Massey who acted similar scenes in *Crossroads* almost twelve years ago.

Though *Crossroads* attempted to integrate black and Asian families in its stories in the 1970s, they were nothing more than stereotypes (black juvenile delinquent, Asian girl in conflict with her father). However, unlike *Coronation Street*, the series continued to employ black and Asian actors and actresses on a regular basis right up to its demise in 1988. In 1982 Dorothy Hobson stated:

> *Crossroads* has been anxious to reflect the culural and ethnic

groups in the area and has had a number of black and Asian families and characters in its storylines. Currently it has the character of Mac, the black garage mechanic who is working at the motel garage and becoming increasingly more important in storylines.[6]

Carl Andrews joined the cast of *Crossroads* as Joe 'Mac' MacDonald in the late 1970s, and played the role for a number of years. However, in 1980 he made the following complaint: "They filmed a big wedding for me. I have the photo of it. But they decided against showing it."[7] His wife, Trina, was played by Merdelle Jordine.

Throughout the 1980s other black and Asian characters featured prominently in *Crossroads*. For example, Sneh Gupta was seen as motel receptionist Rashida Malik, Dorothy Brown played sports instructress Lorraine Baker for several years and, towards the end of its run, Ashok Kumar played Ranjit, the teenage boyfriend of Beverley Grice.

One other black performer who was seen in *Crossroads* towards the end of its run was Sharon Rosita. She made a brief appearance in one episode as a kitchen worker, but you had to look hard to recognise the actress who had previously been seen in a prominent role in Channel Four's successful soap opera *Brookside* in the mid-1980s. In the summer of 1984 Sharon joined the cast of *Brookside* as Kate Moses, who came from a working-class background, and worked as a nurse at the local hospital. In the series she shared a house with friends Sandra Maghie and Pat Hancock. During the siege of their house in 1985, Kate helped her two friends to escape, but was murdered by the psychotic gunman who had held them all hostage. This incident recalled earlier stereotypes of black people in British and Hollywood films who sacrificed themselves for the white heroes and heroines (cf Paul Robeson in *The Proud Valley* and Sidney Poitier in *The Defiant Ones*). Kate was buried on 13 August 1985, and at her funeral we were introduced to her family, who were presented as middle-class and nothing like working-class Kate. The death of Kate Moses was unnecessary and unpleasant. For over a year, Sharon Rosita had given a fine performance as the likeable, friendly Kate. Both the actress and the character she portrayed deserved more attention from the scriptwriters. Here was a talented actress who promised so much, but she was never given an opportunity to develop her character. The insensitivity of the scriptwriters towards Kate, and the miscasting of her family, is one of the major flaws in what is undoubtedly one of Britain's most exciting and stimulating soap operas. However, as far as its representation of black people is concerned, its track record is as poor as *Coronation Street*'s. Since Kate's death, there haven't been any significant black characters in *Brookside*. Avril, played by Camilla Blanche, who had a brief 'romance' in Barbados, not Brookside Close, with Pat Hancock shortly after Kate's death, was merely a cameo appearance.

Sharon Rosita.
Photo courtesy
of Channel 4

Kate Moses – murdered by psychotic gunman in Brookside

It was television producer Julia Smith who decided the time was right to bring the working-class soap opera into the 1980s. The result was *EastEnders* which was first seen on BBC1 on 19 February 1985. Said Smith: "Our East End setting was chosen for the diversity of its past – the strong 'culture' it has, and the multi-racial community that has developed." Since it began, *EastEnders*' mix of social realism and melodrama has proved enormously

127

popular with the British public. Its original cast included a variety of black and Asian charcters such as the Carpenter family (father Tony, played by Oscar James, and his son Kelvin, played by Paul J Medford) and the shopkeepers Naima and Saeed Jeffrey (played by Shreela Ghosh and Andrew Johnson). Later, Sally Sagoe joined the cast as Tony's wife Hannah, and Judith Jacob as social worker Carmel.

However, with the exception of Carmel, all these characters have since disappeared from the series, most of them amidst controversy. Oscar James commented: "Having a black family in a top show has helped show that blacks are not alien beings." However, before he left the series in 1987, he pointed out that "the powers that be do not think I am interesting enough. Is it because I am a member of the ethnic minority? How often do you see Paul J Medford being publicised? Or Asian actress Shreela Ghosh? It's as though the BBC are playing us down. I can't believe the white majority of the public are against blacks being stars. They don't give a damn."[8]

More outspoken than James was Shreela Ghosh. Before she left the cast in 1987 she said:

I keep playing scenes week in, week out which have no substance, and I don't think they've successfully merged Naima into the series. I'm underused and undervalued. In one scene, for instance, I come into the laundrette and Pauline's supposed to show me how to use a washing machine. I haven't just stepped off a boat, for chrissakes!. . . We're a political football for Julia Smith, a trump card over all the soaps – a few black faces, one over on Phil Redmond (creator and executive producer of *Brookside*). The BBC is inherently racist. I work in a building with a thousand people and I see maybe ten black faces. Most of them work in the canteen!. . . A good black script needs a good black director. Time and time again you have sympathetic white directors who don't have enough knowledge. There's a dearth of black writers, black technicians. Things have to change and I have to play a part in that – making a noise, sticking up for what we want and not handing responsibility over to other people.[9]

For the first time on British television an Asian actress had played a major role in a soap opera on a regular basis, and exposed the frustrations she continually faced while playing a character who was basically unrealisic, in storylines that were sometimes racist. Shreela's dilemma gives us an insight into the world of black and Asian performers in contemporary British television soap opera. Perhaps if Granada television had had the foresight to continue employing Thomas Baptiste and Barbara Assoon in *Coronation Street* in the 1960s, the situation today might be different. However, like Baptiste and Assoon, black and Asian performers in British soap opera continue to be, in the words of Shreela Ghosh, "underused and undervalued".

Notes

(1) H.V.Kershaw *The Street Where I Live* (Book Club Associates, 1981) p 170–71

(2) John Stevenson *Press Release for The Brothers McGregor* (Granada Television, 1985)

(3) Angela Bruce *The Voice* February 21 1987

(4) Lisa Lewis *TV Times* December 1–7 1984

(5) Margaret Forward *The Sun* September 8 1977

(6) Dorothy Hobson *Crossroads: The Drama of a Soap Opera* (Methuen, 1982)

(7) Carl Andrews *The Guardian* November 3 1980

(8) Oscar James *The Sun* November 15 1986

(9) Shreela Ghosh *New Musical Express* November 7 1987, reprinted in this collection

EMPIRE ROAD

The popular drama series set in a Birmingham suburb returns to the screen. *Radio Times* takes a look at some of the folk who live there:

EVERTON BENNETT
played by NORMAN BEATON

The prosperous West Indian 'godfather' of *Empire Road* arrived in England from Guyana 20 years ago. Everton is proud of his achievements and of the respect he commands within the West Indian community. Less admirably, he has been known to refer to his Asian neighbours as 'Coolies' and to the Rastafarian youths in his area as 'Jigaboos'.

HORTENSE BENNETT
played by CORINNE SKINNER-CARTER

Hortense, Everton's loyal and loving wife, runs an immaculate house and never serves her family less than three good meals a day. She takes her role as the godfather's wife very seriously – some would say too seriously. But sometimes she yearns for the good old days in Guyana – when she didn't have to worry about keeping one step ahead of the neighbours.

MARCUS BENNETT
played by WAYNE LARYEA

Marcus Bennett, Everton's 20-year-old son, has grown up in Birmingham. He likes the music of Bob Dylan, Bob Marley and

Joan Armatrading. A rebel with an eye for a pretty face, Marcus has fallen in love with a young Asian girl, Ranjanaa. Marcus runs a boxing class for deprived kids in *Empire Road* – but his dream remains to visit and live in New York.

RANJANAA KAPOOR
played by NALINI MOONASAR

Ranjanaa, Marcus' 18-year-old girlfriend, arrived in Birmingham 12 years ago from Uganda. With her mother dead, Ranjanaa helps her father at the Asian Sweet Centre. She likes Kate Bush and punk music – but having been brought up as a Hindu, regards herself as Indian, not English. Her father bitterly opposes her relationship with Marcus.

Radio Times, 18–24 August 1979

Naseem Khan meets the cast of *Empire Road* Usually new comedy programmes slip on to the screen like plastic ducks into the bath, with a mild splash of jovial pre-publicity. No great claims are made for them except that a good time might be had by all. From the beginning *Empire Road*, the black *Coronation Street* as it was inevitably dubbed, had a heavier load to carry. "Unlike so much of TV drama today," its producer went on record as saying, "*Empire Road* is contemporary."

"It may well be," declared *Time Out*, "the first drama series that black people can watch on television without feeling embarrassed or angry." "This is no black *Coronation Street*," said the Jamaican *Weekly Gleaner*, going straight for the bull. "Rather a down-to-earth appraisal of the struggles of West Indians and Asians in Britain." On the other hand, would-be reassuring sounds emerged from the pre-publicity. It might be black, but it wouldn't be 'political' or 'heavy'. Its intention was to 'amuse and entertain'.

Given the pioneering position of *Empire Road* – the first series conceived and written by a black writer for a black cast – the nervousness is only too understandable. It was reflected in the series itself: in a tentative approach by the series writer, Michael Abbensetts; by an overlarding with jolly 'West Indian style' music; and above all by the fact that there were only five half-hour episodes that were shown on BBC2 at the unsociable hour of 6.50pm in the Further Education slot.

Nevertheless, given all these disadvantages, it is to the BBC's credit that they immediately recognised the quality and potential of *Empire Road*. nor did they wait for the ratings. Before episode one even appeared on the screen they had commissioned ten more. The new series has moved from its somewhat Cinderella time to the peak time of 8pm.

Empire Road is no ordinary sitcom or soap opera. The claims made for it have been massive. How, I wondered, did the actors involved in it now feel? Were they nonplussed? Did they feel that what they were doing had answered expectations? And had the experience of it affected them?

For a start, all the four actors I spoke to were in no way surprised. They had known in their bones that *Empire Road* was special. "It is perhaps the best TV series I have been in", said Norman Beaton decisively, a statement that with his experience carries weight. "And people enjoyed the second series perhaps more than anything else they'd ever worked on."

"The series itself was long overdue," declared Corinne Skinner-Carter, Beaton's long-suffering screen wife. "It's always been a white version of black people before. People who know how things are, watched it and said, 'Ah! At last'. People who didn't know, said, 'Oh!. . .It's like that?!' I always thought it would show people a little bit how we feel, as opposed to how they think we feel."

Soft-voiced Nalini Moonasar, who plays the apple of discord between the West Indian and Asian families, was suitably lyrical in her response. "The whole feel while making it was wonderful! You felt like something brand-new was happening. Everybody was really happy to be there. There was a feeling that it was all going to burst out into a . . .wonderful sunflower, or something!" Young Wayne Laryea, who plays Beaton's son and Nalini's suitor, was more soberly positive. "It was a unique experience to be involved in a series of black plays by a black author."

"It's a kind of window that you can look through on to black lives," said Horace Ove, the black film-maker who has directed three of the ten new episodes. "It's a real breakthrough." Unanimous as all the actors are about *Empire Road*, it's clear that for all of them it has a different significance. That is only to be expected. The four of them range from their mid-20s to mid-40s. Wayne was born here; the others came from Guyana and

*Corinne
Skinner–Carter*

Trinidad. Their experience ranges from the school blackboard to show business to stage school.

Norman Beaton, for instance, sees the series in the context of a long and considerable commitment to black theatre. Beaton – Everton Bennett, *Empire Road's* testy 'Godfather' – is arguably Britain's premier black actor. While notching up achievements like the Variety Club's Actor of the Year Award, he still has a perceptive eye to the stepchild situation which black writers and performers have so long occupied. "For years and years," he said forcefully, "producers and directors have been saying that there are no black writers and no black actors or black directors. What *Empire Road* has done is to expose this as a total and utter red herring. The combination of the BBCs expertise and the fact that one can assemble a company like *Empire Road*, and that one has a writer like Abbensetts and a director like Ove, glaringly suggests the ethnic minorities are grossly unrepresented in the media. And that, come 1981 and the revision of TV franchises, there has to be a major rethink by people in control of the media and their finances to redress this balance."

Corinne Skinner-Carter has had a similarly long experience, and knows many of the frustrations that Beaton does. From

Trinidad, she worked as a dancer until, as she engagingly said, she thought, 'Uh, uh – getting too old to kick up your legs', and took drama classes. She is in addition a qualified teacher, and teaches Caribbean dance in a local youth club on a voluntary basis. For her, *Empire Road* was important for redressing the white-orientated bias of television, but she is not uncritical of it. "I didn't like the first three episodes for a start. The trouble was that Abbensetts had only five episodes and he was trying to push everything in. And there was a lack in the first series – the nasty side of it, you could say. The pressures on the black community are shown more clearly in the new series, as opposed to the joviality."

"The new series has put Abbensetts in a position to get his teeth into his subject," Norman Beaton explained. "There was nothing wrong with the first series except that it was approached in a tentative manner. The new series has given Abbensetts the opportunity to expand on the characters, to flesh them out."

"But writers don't like writing for women – even Michael," said Corinne regretfully. "I've always accused him of being a chauvinistic pig. The women in *Empire Road* are passive. I'm only there because Norman must have a wife – because if he wants a cup of coffee he can't make it for himself!"

Nalini Moonasar has no such dissatisfaction with her role. She plays Ranjanaa, the young Indian girl with whom Everton's son falls in love, much to the fury of both parents. "I looked at the part and thought, 'That part is written for me!' I just felt her totally, I loved her! I played her with feeling." In fact, landing the part of Ranjanaa must have been close to Nalini's dream. She came to England as Miss Guyana (an image she would now rather forget), longing to be involved in 'the world of English drama and Olivier and so on'. She'd acted a lot in Guyana ever since her debut as Baby Jesus at the age of four; but she had no experience in Britain.

"Suddenly I realised I was coloured and it was difficult, I never thought of that in Guyana."

Wayne Laryea, who plays Marcus (Nalini's suitor) has yet another view of the series. The son of a Ghanaian father and English mother, born in London, he has no Caribbean connection. "I drew on my own experiences growing up here for Marcus. There is a big cultural gap. It's difficult for second-generation children to maintain the balance between the two cultures. And that's another reason why *Empire Road* is important."

All agree, however, that the second series is a strong development: but that even though it might have teeth, it still doesn't forget its smile. Another difference is in directors. This second series has three – Peter Jefferies, Michael Custance and Horace Ove, who is himself from the West Indies. It was the first time that any of them had been directed on television by a black director. "Oh my gosh!" said Corinne expressively, "He was a picture guy! He was so concerned with how his picture would look. He was more concerned with mood than words. I remember once 'Marcus' asked him for a line to go with a movement Horace wanted, and Horace yelled, 'I don't want lines . . . I want emotion!'"

Ove himself, best-known for his film *Pressure*, had not been keen on being involved in *Empire Road*. "Frankly, I did not like the first lot that went out very much. But I got interested when I read the new lot: they dealt with real life up to a certain extent."

He is certain that, being a West Indian, he got better performances out of the cast. "You see, when West Indian actors go on television they react, and clean up their accents, and lose out on their rhythm and style. English directors will tend to suggest English motivations to them, and they create something else out of it."

What Ove tried to do, he said, was to relate the script and emotions in it to life back home. It worked, particularly for Corinne and Norman. "I got something out of all the directors," said Corinne, "But Horace got me to relax in my body as opposed to the way the English make you work." "Clearly he was in touch with all the unwritten lines in Abbensetts's world," said Norman judiciously. "It was a joy working with a West Indian director. But having said that, I am not knocking the other two directors, who made an equal contribuiton from their own perspective."

Their younger colleagues agreed. Even though Ove might have brought another dimension, they saw it as a variation.

"Basically all the directors were very understanding: each presented a different mood," felt Nalini. "All the directors were excellent," Wayne said firmly, "but since Horace was from the Caribbean he added different shades." The contrast between the three styles of all the directors promises to be one of the most interesting aspects of the second series.

Taken to its logical conclusion, the kind of chemistry that the four actors of *Empire Road* describe so warmly – brought about by the conjunction of black writer, actors and (on occasion) director – must lead to certain questions. Norman Beaton may complain, as he does, that "the Ayckbourns, Stoppards, Mercers of this country don't write parts for black actors: it's as if they're colour blind." But is it desirable that they should, when all four actors claimed they were able to give more to a black script? And it is only recently that white Michael Hastings got dusted up for his West Indian comedy *Gloo Joo*.

"I turned down *Gloo Joo*" Beaton said, "because of its lack of veracity in every area of importance. If a white man," he went on, "is going to write parts for black people, then he has to be absolutely true."

"No," said Wayne Laryea, "It's all right. In the end you're just writing about people, aren't you? It can be just as valid, in a different way. But it's wrong if all there is is white people writing about black people."

In a way he put his finger on it. Black writers have undoubted difficulty in presenting subjects from their own experience both on stage and television. White promoters find the product hard to understand in their own frame of reference, and are unconvinced of its general market value. "Anything to do with Asians or blacks is considered uncommercial unless we're leaping around like lunatics in *Black Mikado* or *Kwa-Zulu*", said Beaton scathingly.

Naseem Khan, *Radio Times*, 23 August 1979

COLOUR TELEVISION

There's nothing unusual about Westbourne Road. It's a quiet little street in Handsworth, Birmingham; and during the day, when the children are at school, it's almost deserted except for the occasional customer going into the tiny grocery shop on the corner. But Westbourne Road is about to become one of the best-known streets in Britain, because it is the site of BBC2's new series, *Empire Road*.

Empire Road began when Guyanese playwright Michael

Abbensetts went to Birmingham for the filming of his play *Black Christmas*.

> I went to stay with a friend in Handsworth, and it struck me that the atmosphere was very different from London. It was more relaxed. Everybody seemed to have more time, and it was easy to see what people's problems were. It was very mixed: blacks, whites and Asians living next door to each other. And you could hear all of them talking in the same Brummie accent. All that happens in London, but in Birmingham I could see it with greater clarity.

The result was *Empire Road*, which is the story of a group of West Indians and Asians living in a surburban street in Birmingham. The series is centred upon the doings of West Indian landlord Everton Bennett, played by Guyanese actor Norman Beaton. Two relationships provide most of the action in the series – the relationship between Everton Bennett and his brother-in-law Walter, which is comic, and the relationship between Everton's son Marcus and his Asian girlfriend Ranjanaa, which is romantic. Just as in the real-life Westbourne Road, the people in the street are drawn from all over the West Indies, Asia and Britain.

The series went in to production during the spring of this year. As it happened, the first of the filming to take place out on location was that of a street party with which the first episode ends. For the occasion Westbourne Road burst into a blaze of flags and bunting, and the filming of the episode took place in the atmosphere of a real street party. There was an all-girl steel band on a truck, there were food stalls and prizes, there was Norman Beaton telling stories, and, to top it all, there was the story of *Empire Road* being performed in front of the very people who had inspired it.

The residents of Westbourne Road remember the event with some enjoyment. The Asian couple who run the corner shop described it as a "lot of fun. A real holiday for the children".

But it wasn't all fun. A few doors up from the shop is the house which served as the television home of landlord Everton Bennett. On the day that I went to call, its Jamaican owner was leaning on the garden gate surveying the street with much the same air of proprietorial assurance that Bennett displays in the series. Like

Bennett, he doesn't mince words. "Never again," he said with relish. "Since that BBC crowd came I've been exposed to so much jealousy in this street that I feel like moving out." As he spoke, I was conscious that we were being observed from behind the lace curtains on either side and across the street. For a moment it was uncannily like being in one of the episodes.

Later on, when I described this incident to Norman Beaton, he laughed out loud. "That's nothing," he said. "I was just knocking off work one night, and a man came up to me and right out of the blue he said: 'You ought to be filming this kind of thing in another street you know. We're all respectable here'."

Comments of that kind were a reflection of one of the difficulties that the production team faced in casting *Empire Road*. One of the main storylines is the romance between the young Asian girl, played by Nalini Moonasar,and the landlord's son, played by Wayne Laryea. This relationship was the source of a great deal of controversy, even before the start of the series. Asian leaders objected to incidents like the two lovers kissing on screen. According to producer Peter Ansorge, "The idea was to find a girl from one of the schools in the area, and we found a number of them, but when we described the plot, it always turned out that their families wouldn't let them do it."

Eventually the part went to Nalini Moonasar, who doesn't come from the Indian sub-continent or East Africa, but, like Michael Abbensetts and Norman Beaton, from Guyana. That part was the most difficult to cast because, contrary to the conventional wisdom, it wasn't hard to find good black actors to fill the parts. On the other hand, the company as a whole came from an intriguing variety of backgrounds. Joe Marcell and Trevor Butler came from an orthodox drama-school and repertory background. But Vincent Taylor, playing the young tearaway Royston, was an O-level pupil at a local school, while Corinne Skinner-Carter was an actress-turned-school-teacher, who had to take time off from her junior school in London's Hackney to play the part. Rosa Roberts (Miss May) was a club entertainer from Leeds.

The real odd-man-out in the cast, however, was Wayne Laryea, who started his acting career in a children's serial made in Hollywood and went on to present a children's puppet programme on ITV. Apart from Mellan Mitchell, who plays the Asian father, Wayne was the only one of the regular cast who was not a West

Indian. His mother is English and he was born and brought up in London. He had to learn Birmingham and West Indian accents from scratch.

Wayne described the relationship between the actors as "the best I'd ever experienced. We felt this was something new, and something very important to us as black actors. We did unusual things, like staying on the set and watching each other's scenes. And it was all very friendly. Nobody trying to upstage the others. It was really nice. But we all owe a debt of gratitude to Norman Beaton. He helped me personally with the accents and the mannerisms, and he was the anchor that held us all together."

Beaton himself was modest about his role. "I came to *Empire Road* with a larger-than-life reputation, having just won the Variety Club's Actor of the Year Award, and that sort of thing is always difficult to justify. My character, Everton Bennett, was the pivot around which most of the scenes revolved, and it was an enormous responsibility in purely acting terms. I had to be there every day, and I had to produce my best every day. If that meant that the rest of the cast had to work at the same level of intensity, it's the only claim I have to be regarded in that light. All I was doing was my job."

To judge by the response of the audiences who've seen previews of *Empire Road* so far, the entire team has done a successful job. One of the episodes was shown recently at the Edinburgh Television Festival and was greeted by television professionals as a breakthrough in the treatment of the ethnic minorities on television. Author Michael Abbensetts hopes, however, that it won't be seen merely as a black version of other television soap operas. "It is a soap opera, and I wrote it to appeal on a popular level, but I think it says something about the real lives of West Indian and Asian people living in British cities."

There is no doubt about the popular appeal of the series. The BBC has already scheduled another ten episodes; Abbensetts is busy writing them.

The one man who reacts warily and with caution of the claims being made for *Empire Road* is producer Peter Ansorge. "It's certainly the first drama series on television which will present West Indians and Asians as ordinary people rather than as problems or lovable clowns, but we made this as a drama series which is meant to entertain people like any other drama series, and we hope it will do just that."

Mike Phillips, *Radio Times*,

Norman Beaton

THE RACE IS ON

They couldn't have made *Empire Road* twenty years ago, when I was a teenager. Since then two things have changed dramatically. One is the attitude on television towards black people; the other is the atmosphere in the areas of Britain where most immigrants have settled.

Traditionally, television has presented black people as problems or victims, rather than as people who are interesting in themselves. Witness the endless stream of documentaries about the problems of race, about blacks and the National Front, and so on.

On the lighter side, most of the jokes in series like *Curry and Chips* or *Love Thy Neighbour*, were based on name-calling between the races. But the truth was that until Rudolph Walker

140

said the word on television, no West Indian ever used terms like 'honky' and there is still no widely accepted term of abuse for whites in West Indian slang.

So the situation was unreal – a television fantasy about the relationships between blacks and whites.

In *Empire Road*, which begins on Tuesday there is no excitement over skin colour as such. The relationships are nearly all between black people themselves and there are no easy caricatures at which to poke fun.

This is much more like the real-life Empire Roads all over Britain where blacks and whites live side by side without the kind of fuss so often highlighted on TV.

Both the star and the storyline of the TV *Empire Road* will be familiar. The main character is a West Indian landlord, played by Norman Beaton, who starred in *The Fosters* and the stories revolve around the various members of his family.

But *Empire Road* differs from any of the shows which have featured immigrants because it is closer to the reality of how West Indians and Asians live in Britain today.

For instance, the street has a vigorous communal life; the landlord is a man of independence and authority and, in day-to-day terms, there isn't much conflict, or even personal contact between blacks and whites.

On the other side of the coin, the serial pulls no punches when it comes to mentioning unemployment among young blacks or the problems created by the racialism that immigrants face in their daily lives.

In one of the later episodes, two of the teenage characters get into a fight at a club, and the story shows the hostility and resentment one of them feels towards all the authorities he's ever encountered.

All that has the flavour of reality but, from a personal point of view, what strikes me most strongly about *Empire Road* is how well it illustrates the changes that have taken place in immigrant life since I first arrived here from the West Indies in 1954.

Then there was no West Indian landlord like Everton Bennett, no black ladies running chip shops – and reggae music hadn't even been invented. My family lived in a small flat at the top of a house in Islington and what I remember most is the feeling of isolation.

141

Racial abuse and assaults were a common feature of everyday life; simply going out to the shops or the cinema could be an ordeal. In those days housing, rather than employment, was the big problem.

Most of the people we knew got jobs fairly quickly on the railways or the buses but finding somewhere to live could be a weary and humiliating grind.

Since then, as we see in *Empire Road*, immigrants have either moved on to council lists or bought their own houses.

Now finding a job is the main headache for young West Indians, a fact which says a great deal about the changing nature of race relations.

It may be hard to believe, when you read about the activities of the National Front, but in comparison with those days there's a lot less overt racism in the streets, and nowadays it's far easier for blacks and whites to meet and mingle.

In my day we took white hostility for granted. Today, young blacks resent discrimination more directly, largely because they're brought up to different expectations. This is a theme that features in all the *Empire Road* stories.

Norman Beaton, as the landlord, represents a generation which took on the hostility and, in its own eyes, won the battle.

For him, the evidence that he's triumphed is his houses, his shops and the fact that he can go back to the Caribbean for a holiday paid for out of his savings.

To the generation represented by his son all this means very little. His battle with the background which has shaped his own life – school, employers – and the attitudes of the older generation, like his father, and the father of his Asian girlfriend who dislikes his daughter associating with anyone of another religion.

Spelling out these issues might make *Empire Road* sound grim, but that's the last thing it is. Describe aloud some of the characters in *Coronation Street* – three nosey and pathetic OAPs, a snooty landlady presiding over a depressed and grimy area of high unemployment – and you'll see what I mean.

Everton Bennett is probably the most convincing West Indian character yet to appear on television. He's mean, bad-tempered, intelligent, kind-hearted, convivial and grumpy all at the same time. Just like a real person.

142

In that sense his personality has a universal appeal which could be as strong as the attraction Ena Sharples had for the early *Coronation Street* audiences.

I don't know whether *Empire Road* can hope to change relations between the races in Britain for the better. But I do know that it is evidence that the black community is producing some good writers, actors and stories.

Mike Phillips, *Daily Mail*, 28 October 1978

BLACK SOAP IS A WASHOUT

"Hey mum turn over *EastEnders* is on!" Some of us love it others hate it but whatever your opinion there can be no doubt which programme is carrying the swing in England. Well what about a black soap? Why haven't black programme-makers moved in this direction and basically cleaned up on the ratings? Do we have the resources to create a black soap?

Every Tuesday and Thursday 19 million people sit down to watch BBC's *EastEnders*. With the exception of Kelvin and his father the series is in essence a white soap opera. These actors should really have the option to act in a black soap opera, created and produced by black artists who would use the format to project the richness and complexity of the black community.

What is preventing such a project materialising first lies in the attitude of many black writers who have not freed their minds from what can be called the 'victim syndrome' – the idea that plays, poems and television must project black people as suffering victims, begging the 'liberal conscience' for mercy. This was acute in the early seventies when plays and documentaries would only project black people as angry or beating their chest at a white society that had caused injustice.

James Berry a leading Jamaican poet explains: "I have decided that I will have no truck with images that only see black people as victims. We must demand to see the full glory of ourselves. A black soap would be an exciting idea. Those writers who are preoccupied with rage at the white man have used their creative energies in the wrong way. What we need are writers who will exalt the black experience and examine its complexity."

Perhaps a more hardhitting reason why we haven't had our

share of good soap, is the racism of BBC and ITV (IBA). Leading writer Cas Phillips looks back to the days of ITV's *Love Thy Neighbour*, which according to him, "gave black people a spurious image and was never honest about the black experience, which was always measured in relation to whites."

However, white director and programmer Ken Slater argues that white companies are desperate for good black writing: "During the social unheaval of the sixties in England and America, women emerged as the new generation of people that the media would open its doors to. The social unheavals of the 80s had resulted in a greater interest in black people."

Another reason why soap has turned to black suds is the 'Straight Jacket' approach of many black programme-makers who feel that to be washed in black soap will harm the black communities political integrity. All that can be said of that is 'hogwash'. We all love a good story and why not? It's nothing to be ashamed of. There are many reasons why the soap opera format is so popular. The main one is the fact that it examines a whole range of 'human' interests that are commonplace to everyone irrespective of their background. The stories of 'betrayal', 'jealousy', 'shame' and 'love' are fascinating to all. The reason that *Dynasty* and *Dallas* can sell so well is not because the government in some sort of clandestine manner are trying to dupe the people. It is because the fantasies can be related to, even if we can't live like Joan Collins.

The only real attempt at a 'black soap' was back in the seventies with the BBC series *Empire Road*. The story of the 'Empire' coming home to Handsworth. Although it was beset with teething problems, given the disaster of the incestuous *No Problem* sitcom 'lets look at each others belly-button and have a laugh', *Empire Road* was ahead of its time.

When looking at good soaps it does seem ironic that as 19 million people in England watch the white orientated *EastEnders*, over 80 million Americans watch the top rating TV *The Cosby Show*. This programme captures the interest of black and white because as, black producer Trevor Phillips argues: "It is a show that gives you the black experience without needing to say that it is black. It is the biggest property in America because it is popular without compromising its integrity."

For those of us who feel that they need the reassurance of a political 'jerk off', then the structure of the soap opera has been seen to be one of the better mediums for political comments. The plight of being unemployed in Liverpool was richly conveyed in the early episodes of *Brookside* where Bobby's whole notion of his manhood and experience as head of the family is seriously challenged when he was out of work. Alan Bleasdale's *Boys from the Blackstuff* used the popular idiom again to look at the question of unemployment.

There are dangers with the 'soap' format in that it is open to stereotyping but perhaps more complex is the danger of distorted romance. This is a charge placed against *Coronation Street* and *The Cosby Show*. It is argued that in the former, working-class people are static, representing the post-war 'cloth cap' white working-class who were basically content with their lot and leaves any political agitation to an articulate, 'Ken Barlow'. It is true that Manchester now has few cobbled streets and more people watch television and go to nightclubs than to the local 'Rovers Return'. The absence of black people is more evidence that the nostalgia of *Coronation Street* will mean this serial will gradually become a 'history' piece and will in time be superceded by something better. This something better is presently *EastEnders* but it could so easily be a black soap.

The question of how a black soap can be created in England, when there is a lack of good black producers needs to be addressed. Experience will only come through practice. The young black writers such as Jacqueline Rudet and directors such as Paulette Randall are entitled to graduate to television. A pool of writers would be necessary to write a well crafted script. The excellent *Slice of Life*, a woman's drama shows that there is talent to write popularist programmes. From the old guard, writers like John Agard who has a great reservoir of wit, Tundi Ikoli, James Berry and Cas Phillips are all people who could have a positive input.

In terms of the subject matter it would be interesting to follow *The Cosby Show* format and produce a family serial that examines the complexities and hopes of a black family.

The advantages of starting with a family drama is in terms of cost and production. This kind of drama relies more on the skill of the actors, than a soap with higher production values like *EastEnders* which has many characters and different locations.

The family idea would be good not only for production but also in terms of the way in which young people perceive themselves and black families. The image of a 'good' family is one of continuity and stability, even if it's a one-parent family. This is in contrast with images of instability, victim and irresponsibility, so often the result of prior attempts at black programming. The issue here would not be whether the 'black family is breaking down'. To a certain extent this becomes irrelevant. What the main task should be is to use the positive format of the 'family' to extend to everyone the infinite possibilities of the black experience.

Tony Sewell, *The Voice*, 7 December 1985

EASTENDERS

Ask any EastEnder for directions to Albert Square, London Borough of Walford, E20, and they'll tell you: "Straight down Turpin Road Market, turn right into Bridge Street, and there it is, with the Queen Vic pub on the corner."

Ask anyone, and they'll tell you that the two best-known families in the square are the Beales and the Fowlers. "Lived here since the year dot!" *Lou Beale,* in her 70s, is head of a large cockney family. She's plump, loud, funny and sentimental – but can be stubborn, too. Two of Lou's children have stayed in the East End: Pauline and Pete... *Pauline Fowler,* who does the morning shift at the local launderette, is married to *Arthur,* and they have two teenage kids, *Mark* and *Michelle*. They all share Lou's house: 45 Albert Square.

Pauline's twin brother, *Pete,* who has a fruit 'n' veg stall in Bridge Street, lives with his second wife, *Kathy*, and son *Ian* in a flat on the nearby 'Estate'.

Ask anyone about the Beales and the Fowlers, *Den Watts,* for instance, the guv'nor of the Queen Vic, is Pete Beale's best mate (Pete's barrow is right outside the pub). Since the lads were schoolkids, Den's always been on the fiddle, and Pete's always covered for him. S'what mates are for, innit?

Ask anyone who holds that pub together, and they'll say: *"She does! Angie* is no fool." Lately, the publican's wife is starting to wonder if she's the one who's being 'fiddled' by Jack-the-lad Den. Tricky that, seeing as Angie's best mate is Kathy, Pete's wife, and Kathy doesn't lie. It's all a bit tough on Den and Angie's adopted daughter, *Sharon* – piggy-in-the-middle.

There are not many people in Albert Square *Dr Harold Legg* doesn't know – he brought most of them into the world. Lou Beale can't work out why he keeps his surgery in the square, as he moved home out of the district years ago. An old-fashioned, 'family' doctor, he goes back a long way with Lou. He can see right through her and knows, when she's being the battleaxe, that it's all an act so that she can get her own way – which is most of the time!

Dr Legg's cleaning lady, *Ethel Skinner*, lives in the flat above his surgery. She's Lou Beale's greatest friend. You can't miss Ethel: she's always wearing a hat and always followed by her little dog, Willy. She also cleans the pub – when she turns up, that is! She's inclined to get carried away telling fortunes in the market or getting conned into doing laundry for Lofty.

Lofty Holloway occupies the flat above Ethel. Funny lad, Lofty. He's got the gift of the gab all right: can charm the birds off the trees. But he keeps vanishing – for days on end. Lofty does work now and then. Like three sessions a week behind the bar at the pub – cash in hand, of course.

Ali and *Sue Osman*, and nine-month-old baby *Hassan*, live in a council flat on the run-down side of Albert Square. They run Al's Cafe in Bridge Street, just across the road from the Vic and frequented by the market traders. Ali, a Turkish Cypriot, is likeable but lazy, and gambles away half the caff's takings, which doesn't keep Sue in the best of moods. She's sharp-tongued at the best of times. And that's what gets up Kathy Beale's nose.

In the room above Sue and Ali's (and sharing the bathroom) is *Mary Smith* and her nine-week-old daughter *Annie*. No-one in the square is convinced she's going to be able to manage. Lou says that Mary's a bit young to be bringing up a child alone. Sue Osman reckons she clutters up the bathroom.

Ask anyone if there's a builder, decorator, handyman in the square and they'll point you in the direction of number 3, where *Tony Carpenter* lives. Or *will* live when he finishes 'doing it up'. Meanwhile, he sleeps in his van. Tony is about to get a divorce, and his wife is convinced he won't stay in Walford. Tony has no staying power, she believes.

Kelvin, Tony's son, is studying for his GCEs and CSEs. He could do without the aggro between his parents. He's also got problems with Michelle Fowler and Sharon Watts, the rivals for his affections. Opposite Al's Cafe is the Foodstore run by two young Bengalis, *Saeed* and *Naima Jeffery*, who live round the corner in the square. Their marriage was hastily arranged because Saeed's parents had to return to India and wanted someone to keep the business going. But shop work is very new and confusing for them – rather similar to their relationship. If you ask Lou Beale, she will tell you the shop carries "too much foreign muck".

And there are newcomers in the square, too. *Debs* and *Andy* are working-class professionals (she works in a bank, he's a children's nurse). But to most of the inhabitants of Albert Square they're 'outsiders': posh, even. Lou says Debs is too bossy by half – really 'stuck up'. Andy makes excuses for her.

Families and family life play a large part in everyday happenings in Albert Square. Who's doing what, to whom, and where is the constant chat of the neighbourhood. Gossip, intrigue and scandal are high on the list of daily events. Ask anyone . . .

Tony Holland, *Radio Times*, 16–22 February 1985

The representation of blacks on British television needs further discussion but *EastEnders* does seem to be attempting to move beyond the position that race is a problem (with the corollory that it is blacks who actually create the problem) and the presentation of black characters as victims, forced to suffer the abuses of racism. The sense of excess referred to earlier works to the programme's advantage here. *EastEnders* certainly benefits from the number of black characters led by a challenging performance from Oscar James as Tony and from the range of races represented – Bengali, West Indian, Turkish. No single character is left to carry the burden of race as Jonah briefly did in *Brookside* and as Kate does now.

In addition, the melodramatic relish of *EastEnders* allows the black characters to take up active and dramatic roles. This sometimes occurs when race is not being directly presented as an issue. Tony's relationship with his son or his brief involvement with Angie have a striking generosity while the tense quarrels and reconciliations between Naima and Saeed are set against a whole range of successful/unsuccessful marriages in the pro-

*Gossip, intrigue and scandal high on the list of daily events in Albert
Square*

gramme. On the other hand, when race is at issue the
melodramatic bent of the programme can be to the advantage of
the black characters. The routing of Nick was one of the few
occasions on British television when a group of blacks (with Lofty
inevitably tagging along) were seen to make a decision to attack
a white racist and to carry the initiative out successfully. The
beating up of Nick was a dramatic incident, made the more so by
his subsequent departure from the serial, it remains to be seen
whether *EastEnders* can build on what seems to me to be a
hopeful start.

It was not to be expected, however, that the handling of race
would be unproblematic and there are particular problems when
the black characters are set in the context of the community as a
whole. It is not clear yet how far the notion of community is going
to be pushed in *EastEnders*. The response to Hassan's death, for

150

instance, was tentative with different characters offering support out of their own initiative rather than as part of a group response – Lou Beale sure of the correct behaviour at a time of death, the others making their own more uncertain gestures. Nevertheless, *EastEnders* follows the other British serials in trying to root itself in a particular locality, in this case the East End of London rather than Liverpool, Birmingham or the Yorkshire Dales. At the core of the early episodes was the white working-class Beale/Fowler family, headed though by no means dominated by the matriarchal Lou Beale. These characters are in some senses presented as the norm, the 'genuine' *EastEnders*, cockney characters marked by their traditional resilience, good humour and community solidarity. The other characters tend to be defined by their difference from this archetypal East End family – they are potentially at least outsiders through class (Debbie), profession (Dr Legg) or most markedly through race.

Nevertheless, *EastEnders*, while drawing on an image of cockney London, does escape its boundaries. Lou Beale carries considerable moral weight but her responses, though not to be dismissed, are often seen as out-of-date and inappropriate. The cot death episode in which Hassan died presented us with two different modes of grief – Ali's and Sue's – and invited us to be compassionate towards both, in their difference, not in their similarity. The invitation to enter a community is one of the great pleasures offered by serials. It will be interesting to see whether *EastEnders* can construct a community based not on the similarities of human nature (the classic fallback position of soap operas) but on the potentialities of different cultures.

Christine Geraghty, *Marxism Today*, August 1985

If the explicit discourses of class politics are thus rarely visible in *EastEnders*, those of class identity and class difference are certainly emphasised in many of the key relationships and storylines. The same could not, however, be argued in relation to issues of race and ethnicity. Although on one level the serial does represent a multi-cultural community, it has tended to efface cultural differences and inequalities in favour of 'positive images' of inter-racial co-operation. Nevertheless, this process is not without its contradictions.

Perhaps the most significant fact about *EastEnders'* black characters is simply that they exist: compared with other British soaps, and indeed with much British television in general, their mere presence is unusual. Furthermore, the black characters are often given central dramatic roles within the narrative: far from being marginal, they are embedded in its complex network of relationships, and in certain cases (most notably Tony Carpenter) occupy privileged and authoritative positions within it.

On the other hand *EastEnders* could be (and has been) accused of simply reproducing a limited range of racist stereotypes. Thus, until the recent introduction of an Asian doctor, its sole Asian characters were shopkeepers. Naima has been one of the primary representatives of the small business ethic within the serial and has come into conflict with the other characters as a result of her assertive approach to developing her business – although this may not necessarily mean that she has been judged negatively as a result, paricularly since her main business rival has been Den Watts.

However, it is clear that her commitment to her business has not been entirely a matter of choice – as she once said, "Just because I'm Bengali doesn't mean I like working in a shop" – but it has been linked to her desire for economic and personal independence. It would therefore be wrong to suggest that she has been represented as a money-grabbing capitalist, out to exploit the local community for all she can get – and in this sense, she is not an 'Asian shopkeeper' stereotype.

Nevertheless, the implicit equation 'Asian' = 'shopkeeper' is a misrepresentation – as is the more 'positive image' of the Asian doctor. The majority of Asian workers in Britain are in fact employed as unskilled and semi-skilled waged labour. Yet to assess 'stereotypes' in terms of their accuracy to the real world leads to a very reductive form of analysis which ignores the specific constraints and conventions of the genre. In fact, there are very few characters in *EastEnders* employed in waged labour – and this is at least partly a result of the need to maintain narrative complexity and development. If Naima were employed in a factory, it would be far more difficult to involve her in the storyline. One could make a similar argument about the representation of black family life: the collapse of Saeed and Naima's arranged marriage and the break-up of the Carpenter

EastEnders.
Photo courtesy
of BBC

Carmel (Judith Jacob) and Matthew (Steven Hartley) tie the knot

family could be accused of conforming to inaccurate racist stereotypes – although it is clearly one of the requirements of soap opera as a genre that marriages cannot last, and that the narrative must constantly be regenerated by combining the characters in new relationships.

At any one point in the narrative, there are bound to be systematic imbalances in the representation of particular social groups, although this is not to say that these will always remain. The presence of an Asian shopkeeper today does not preclude the introduction of an Asian doctor, or perhaps an Asian publican or an Asian graphic designer in the future. In many ways, the existing characters fail to connect with dominant stereotypes, and even deliberately oppose them: Kelvin, for example, is very far from being a troublesome black youth. Because the black characters in *EastEnders* have to stand in for groups which are themselves extremely diverse, they are bound to be read against a 'background' of racist stereotypes which are constantly being reasserted in the culture at large, and which viewers will inevitably bring to the programme. Particularly for viewers whose social experience does not bring them into contact with black people, they will therefore tend to be highly 'charged'. In this sense, the degree of 'accuracy' of a representation may be less important than the *discourses* which surround it. The crucial question is not whether *EastEnders'* black characters are 'realistic', but how the serial invites its viewers to make sense of questions of ethnicity – and in particular, how it defines ethnic difference and inequality or racism.

In fact, *EastEnders'* stance towards racism is often explicitly didactic. Racist characters such as Dot and Nick Cotton are routinely 'corrected' and attacked for their beliefs by the more authoritative characters. Although there have been a few cases of the other white characters expressing racist views, the vast majority would appear to be completely lacking in prejudice.

Thus, as I have shown, although Lou Beale began life in the serial expressing some hostility towards Saeed and Naima, her attitude appeared to have magically changed by the time Saeed departed for Bangladesh. Yet again, although Pete and Kathy disapproved of Wicksy going out with Naima – and were condemned by him for their prejudiced views – there has been no evidence of racism on their part since that time.

More extreme forms of racism have tended to derive from outside the community, for example in the form of the protection gang which terrorised the 'ethnic minority' characters of Albert Square in the early months of 1986, extorting money and daubing their shops with paint. Yet this storyline was very ambiguous, not least because Beresford, the leading villain, was himself black. Although the harrassment was clearly directed at the black characters, the fact that a black person was carrying it out meant that the racial dimension was simultaneously emphasised and effaced, making for some bizarre contradictions:

BERESFORD: We're acting as agents on behalf of Mr Jesper Scannell, who is offering a new neighbourhood scheme to

154

tradesmen of the minority persuasion, particularly aimed at integrating them into the cultural majority. We live in a desperate racist society. No doubt you've noticed this, sir. I've suffered myself. This may surprise you, but I have suffered, particularly when a boy. An unfortunate trick of colouring and feature giving me a somewhat Hebrew appearance. Sufficiently so that the yobs of my youthful day sought constant pleasure in bouncing my head against a wall. So I know, believe me, I know what our immigrant friends go through. Now, thankfully, Mr Scannell is going to eliminate all this: eliminate petrol poured through letter boxes, excrement smeared on door handles, racist abuse daubed on walls and windows. But this will inevitably incur some heavy expenses.

In response to the harassment, it was Tony Carpenter who assumed the role of black community leader. For him, the issue was clearly to do with race: and when Pete Beale questioned whether Ali Osman (who was another of the victims of the gang) could really be described as black if he was a Turkish Cypriot, Tony asserted that he was still an 'outsider', 'an ethnic minority' – 'To a lot of your people he will never belong. Here again, the police were seen as unable to defend the community, leading Naima to accuse them of racism: "They don't care when it's us".

Nevertheless, as with its representation of class, the serial rarely makes reference to broader structural inequalities – in this case, to institutional racism. Racism is predominantly defined as a question of individual prejudice or discrimination. While this might be regarded simply as a further consequence of the focus on interpersonal relationships which tends to characterise soap opera as a genre, it is also a significant element within the serial's broader 'multi-culturalist' approach. Through their disavowal of individual racial prejudice, the white characters effectively disclaim the inequality between themselves and the black characters, and the possibility that they might benefit from institutional racism. The fact that racism is generally located outside the community or in the prejudices of individual deviant characters thus allows the serial to construct an oasis of multi-racial harmony.

In order to do this, it must also seek to efface the signs of racial difference, to construct white characters with black faces. While the ethnicity of the white characters remains unproblematic, that of the black characters is rarely emphasised. This is largely because each of the 'ethnic minorities' represented in the programme is personified by a few individuals: although Naima and Ali occasionally refer to their families, for example, we rarely see them in the company of large numbers of other characters from the same culture. Thus, if they do bear specific cultural values, they do so as individuals; and they are constantly having to adapt to the values of the dominant white characters.

In an interview conducted shortly before the launch of the serial, the producer, Julia Smith, made a remark which seems to me to encapsulate this 'multi-culturalist' approach very clearly:

> We have got a couple of very nice young Bengali characters whom I think everyone will like, and I hope that people won't even realise they're Bengalis.

In this respect at least, the serial would appear to be premissed on the idea that we all possess an 'essential humanity': if only we would recognise that we are all the same under the skin, the inequalities between us would simply fade away.

David Buckingham, *Public Secrets – EastEnders and its Audience* (British Film Institute 1987)

WE'LL MAKE A DRAMA OUT OF YOUR CRISIS

How much longer can we take this tiresome soap? How much longer can the vaudevillian slapstick of Angie and Den dominate the proceedings? How much longer the Cockney cab driver "Gor blimey stone the cross" stereotypes? How much longer can they sell us the idea of a community when Thatcher's docklands makes that a mythical nonsense? How much longer the pretence at covering 'real, social' issues within a framework that is far from radical, if not downright reactionary? How much longer before we all throw up?

EastEnders held a promise at one time. The promise of a populist human drama; engaging, challenging, entertaining. What once showed great script-writing potential has tended towards caricature – the more interesting characters relegated to sidelines. Tabloid culture has dictated the direction of the show – the Anita Dobson and Leslie Grantham exposure in the newspapers, PAs, magazines even *Top of the Pops* – ensuring that those two lead the freakshow, one that is becoming an unwatchable joke.

And what of the cast? What do they feel? The last six months has seen the decimation of the Carpenter family, the first black family featured on a British soap. Opportunities for breaking new ground for black actors, and cutting into stereotypes have been discarded. Sally Sagoe, who played the character of Hannah Carpenter, left amidst a storm of publicity, claiming in a recent interview in the black newspaper *The Voice* that she was sacked for speaking out, "for making my dissatisfaction with the unrealistic stories known". She also said that Leslie Grantham cracked jokes on set about the show's black cast, calling them 'Sooties'.

Oscar James, playing a harassed Tony Carpenter going back to Trinidad, has left the show, fed up with taking a back seat to other stars and tired of script writers with "no idea" how to write stories around black families. With Paul Medford's departure in July, the situation looks bleak for the remaining black cast.

Forging on as shopgirl Naima in *EastEnders*, Shreela Ghosh is anxious about being isolated, though at present Judith Jacob (social worker Carmel) has no plans to leave.

Born in India, Shreela grew up in Calcutta, came to England in 1976 and established herself as a trained Indian classical dancer and actress. I spoke to her shortly before the opening of her East London wine bar, a venture launched with Paul Medford as an 'investment, a nest egg'. Although she is continuing with *EastEnders* Shreela works under no illusions.

"I keep playing scenes week in, week out which have no substance, and I don't think they've successfully merged Naima into the series. I'm underused and undervalued."

She echoes other black cast members in her dissatisfaction with what she sees as unconvincing storylines and "appallingly written scripts. One week Naima's a nice normal character and the next week she turns into a sort of ethnic backlash. You come across stage directions included for a bit of colour, that are just CRAP! In one scene, for instance, I come into the laundrette and Pauline's supposed to show me how to use a washing machine. I haven't just stepped off a boat, for chrissakes!"

Another disturbing incident occurred early in the series when Naima's husband, Said, was portrayed as a pervert. "I think that was grossly irresponsible, putting such an image of an Asian man in a racist society that sees Asian people as aliens. You just don't need that." Shreela and the director Antonia Bird fought against the decision and lost. The actors have no say over their parts, there appears to be no back-up or place to air grievances. "During the Sally Sagoe furore," Shreela continues, "there was very little support – not even a message of sympathy from Julia Smith, the producer, to the black members of the cast. We're a political football for Julia Smith, a trump card over all the soaps – a few black faces, one over on Phil Redmond."

EastEnders publicity has always claimed that its use of black characters shows radical casting, a strong case of postive imagery, yet their appearance has dwindled to the point of sending one back to Bangladesh, one to Trinidad.

"If that's the only way they can get rid of black characters in *EastEnders*, does that mean there's no place for us in society? If you can't fit in you go back home. It's a strong message."

A hefty subtext in a society where deportation and immigration laws are operating with full force, a society where black or Asian people may dream of "going home to a land of milk and honey, but it isn't a reality, a choice. And their children will certainly stay".

Shreela says categorically that "the BBC is inherently racist. I work in a building with a thousand people and I see maybe ten black faces. Most of *them* work in the canteen!"

Do you see anything positive about your character?

"I liked the radical way Naima at first developed," says Shreela, "she started with the traditional image of sari and long wig. I fought with Julia about that because I felt it wasn't an image I wanted to represent, as it wasn't necessarily true. 'But darling', Julia said, 'I want to see you change, for people to see what's happened'. A sari in British society is a barrier – you either think of the woman as dumb, not being able to speak English, or you see her as an exotic goddess. Maybe that portrayal broke down some barriers."

Despite Naima's change to Western clothes, Shreela is quick to stress that "jeans and independence do not go together. It was the break-up of her marriage for her, as it is for a lot of women, which helped her realise her potential. Independence is being able to have the choice."

In this way Shreela is presenting a positive image for Asian women – "when I was at school there were no role models at all. Now I get a lot of letters from Asian girls, some of which are straightforwardly asking how to be an actress and some are cries for help; 'I want to be like Naima, leave home, be independent'. It's important they have someone to write to."

With over 18 million viewers closely following the fortunes of Albert Square each week, it is important that black characters remain to challenge stereotypes or offer role models, but until the structure of the industry changes, there is always the risk of naff scripting. "A good black script needs a good black director," says Shreela, "time and time again you have sympathetic white directors who don't have enough knowledge. There's a dearth of black writers, black technicians."

We're sitting in her East End wine bar which she argues is not just a Yuppie service but also a meeting place for people to write and discuss scripts. "Things have to change and I have to play a part in that – making a noise, sticking up for what we want and not handing responsibility over to other people."

Lucy O'Brien, *New Musical Express*, 11 July 1987

CREDITS AND TRANSMISSION DATES

EMPIRE ROAD

Written by: Michael Abbensetts
Producer: Peter Ansorge
Theme music: Matumbi
Production Company: BBC
Tx dates: 31.10.78–28.11.78 (1st series)
23.8.79–25.10.79 (2nd series)

CAST
Norman Beaton (Everton Bennett); Nalini Moonasar (Ranjanaa); Wayne
Laryea (Marcus Bennett); Corinne Skinner-Carter (Hortense)

EASTENDERS

Producer: Julia Smith
Script editor: Tony Holland
Title music: Simon May & Leslie Osborne
Production Company: BBC
Tx date: 26.2.85–

CAST (of original episode tx.26.2.85)
Anna Wing (Lou Beale); Wendy Richard (Pauline Fowler); Bill Treacher
(Arthur Fowler); Susan Tully (Michelle Fowler); David Scarboro (Mark
Fowler); Peter Dean (Pete Beale) Gillian Taylforth (Kathy Beale); Adam
Woodyatt (Ian Beale); Leslie Grantham (Den Watts); Anita Dobson
(Angie Watts); Letitia Dean (Sharon Watts); Gretchen Franklin (Ethel
Skinner); Leonard Fenton (Dr Legg); John Altman (Nick Cotton); Sandy
Ratcliff (Sue Osman); Nejdet Sahih (Ali Osman); Shreela Ghosh (Naima
Jeffery); Harry Miller (Det Insp Marsh); Brian Hoskin (Mr Chumley)